Her eyes s...

seeking only one person and experiencing
keen disappointment when she couldn't locate
Shane Reynolds. It was still early, and he probably
hadn't arrived yet. People were everywhere, sipping
champagne and chatting easily, but Carrie had never
been good at making small talk.

Her hostess waved at her. "Carrie, you're
positively stunning."

She knew she looked her best. She wanted to make
her meeting with Shane Reynolds a memorable one.
Her gaze skidded across the room, thinking perhaps
she had merely missed him the first time. A glass of
champagne was handed to her. As she raised the
wine to her lips, she spotted a flash of silver from
across the room. The bubbly liquid stayed on her
tongue as her eyes collided with Shane Reynolds's.

A slow, sensuous grin edged up the corners of
his mouth, and he slowly raised his glass in a
silent salute.

Dear Reader,

Welcome to Silhouette. Experience the magic of the wonderful world where two people fall in love. Meet heroines who will make you cheer for their happiness, and heroes (be they the boy next door or a handsome, mysterious stranger) who will win your heart. Silhouette Romances reflect the magic of love—sweeping you away with books that will make you laugh and cry, heartwarming, poignant stories that will move you time and time again.

In the next few months, we're publishing romances by many of your all-time favorites, such as Diana Palmer, Brittany Young, Emilie Richards and Arlene James. Your response to these authors and other authors of Silhouette Romances has served as a touchstone for us, and we're pleased to bring you more books with Silhouette's distinctive medley of charm, wit and—above all—*romance*.

I hope you enjoy this book and the many stories to come. Experience the magic!

Sincerely,

Tara Hughes
Senior Editor
Silhouette Books

DEBBIE MACOMBER
No Competition

Silhouette Romance

Published by Silhouette Books New York

America's Publisher of Contemporary Romance

To my Aunt Paula who loves books as much as I do.
To John who loves my Aunt Paula
And to Sandy and Paula Sharon, loving cousins
and good friends.

SILHOUETTE BOOKS
300 E. 42nd St., New York, N.Y. 10017

Copyright © 1987 by Debbie Macomber

ISBN: 0-373-08512-5

First Silhouette Books printing June 1987

America's Publisher of Contemporary Romance

Printed in the U.S.A.

Books by Debbie Macomber

Silhouette Romance

Silhouette Special Edition

DEBBIE MACOMBER

has quickly become one of Silhouette's most prolific authors. As a wife and mother of four, she not only manages to keep her family happy, but she also keeps her publisher and readers happy with each book she writes.

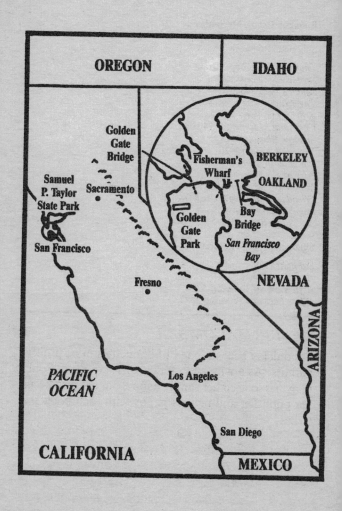

Chapter One

Carrie Lockett carefully backed the fifteen-year-old station wagon to the rear entrance of Dove's Gallery. Shifting the car into park, she hopped out the side door and folded down the back of the wagon to take out the large canvas. She didn't like what she was doing, but the portrait of Camille grinning at her every time she entered her work room was driving Carrie up the wall. All right, she openly admitted it: she was insecure. But who wouldn't be with a twin sister who looked like Camille?

"Darn you, Camille," she muttered disparagingly. Carrie had nothing to blame but her own insecurities.

As an artist, Carrie had yearned to paint her fine-boned, fine-featured sister. Camille was lovely in a delicate, symmetrical way that had brought her admirers in droves. No one could look at Camille without being arrested by her beauty.

Awkwardly balancing the canvas with one hand, Carrie pounded on the rear door of the gallery.

Elizabeth Brandon opened it for her. The older woman's astute gaze narrowed on the dilapidated station wagon. "Darling, are you still driving that... thing?"

It was Elizabeth's opinion that a woman of talent shouldn't be seen in anything so mundane. If it were up to her friend, Carrie would be seated behind the wheel of a Ferrari. Carrie had no objections to that, but the middle-aged vehicle was all she could afford. "It's the only car I have."

"I hope you realize that if that 'thing' was a horse, they'd shoot it."

Carrie managed to smother a laugh. "I suppose. Now do you want to lecture me about my car, or look at this portrait?"

Already Elizabeth's keen eyes were examining the painting. "Darling," she breathed out slowly, "she's exquisite."

"I know," Carrie grumbled. No one would ever guess that the stunning woman in the portrait was the artist's twin sister. Camille's dark hair shone with a luster of the richest sable. Carrie's own mousy reddish-blond hair looked as though Mother Nature couldn't decide what color it should be. Even worse, Carrie had been cursed with a sprinkling of freckles across her nose that stood out like shiny new pennies the minute she hit sunlight. Camille's complexion had been peaches and cream from the time she was a toddler.

"Look at those eyes," Elizabeth continued, her hand supporting her chin. "Such a lovely shade of blue."

Carrie lowered her own greenish-gray ones. Camille's eyes resembled the heavens, and Carrie's looked like dirty swamp water.

"She's intriguing."

Camille was that, all right.

"But I sense a bit of a hellion in all that beauty."

Elizabeth had always been a perceptive woman. One didn't become the proprietor of San Francisco's most elite art gallery without a certain amount of insight.

"Is she anyone I know, darling?"

The way Elizabeth called everyone darling continually amused Carrie. She struggled to hold back a smile. "No, I don't think you would."

"She owes you money?"

"No."

Elizabeth's astute eyes looked directly into Carrie's as a gradual grin formed, bracketing the older woman's mouth. "You've outdone yourself this time. She's fascinating."

"Will it sell?" The question was posed to change the subject. At the moment, Carrie was more concerned with doing away with the irritating portrait than any financial reward.

"I think so."

"Quickly?"

"Someone's coming in this afternoon who might be interested. He's bought several of your other pieces."

Carrie sat on the corner of the large oak desk while Elizabeth directed a young employee to hang the portrait out front.

"This 'someone' who's coming in this afternoon... Is it anyone I know?"

"I don't believe so. Have you heard of Shane Reynolds?"

Carrie wrinkled her nose. The name was oddly familiar, but she couldn't remember where she'd heard it. "Yes, I think I have."

"He's the architect who designed the new Firstbank building."

"Of course. Didn't he just win a plaque or something for that?" She idly rolled a pencil between her fingers, trying to put a face with the name. None came. If his picture had been in the paper, she had missed it.

"Oh darling, you amaze me. Shane was presented the Frank Lloyd Wright annual award. It's the most prestigious honor given to an architect."

"Then he must be good."

"He's single." The statement was accompanied by two perfectly shaped brows arching suggestively.

Carrie shrugged. "So?"

"So let me introduce you."

"Now?" Shock echoed in her voice. "No way, Elizabeth. Look at me." She pushed back the headband that held her curly hair at bay and rubbed her hand down her jean-clad thigh. "I'm a mess."

"Hurry home and pretty yourself up."

"He hasn't got that much time."

Tapping her foot in unspoken reprimand, Elizabeth continued, "I wish you'd stop putting yourself down."

"I'm calling a spade a spade."

"I don't know why you live the way you do. There are plenty of eligible young men in San Francisco. You're an attractive young woman."

"Good try, my friend, but I happen to pass a mirror every now and then. If you want classic beauty then look at the woman in that portrait."

"A man like Shane Reynolds wouldn't be romantically interested in someone like the woman in your painting."

"I know from experience that you're wrong. You stand the two of us together and there's no competition. No man in his right mind would choose me over...her." Carrie nearly spilled out Camille's name which would have been a mistake. During the few years that Carrie had been doing business with the Dove Gallery she'd gone to great lengths to keep her personal life separate from her professional one.

"Shane isn't like other men." Amusement danced briefly in the older woman's gaze while the rest of Elizabeth's face remained stoic.

"Ha," Carrie snorted. "When it comes to a beautiful woman, all men react the same way."

"Have I ever suggested you meet a patron?"

Carrie hedged. Elizabeth wasn't a matchmaker. The other woman's persistence surprised her. "No," she admitted reluctantly.

"There's something about Shane Reynolds I think you'll like. He's enthralled with your work."

"Oh?"

"Besides, he's a bit of a free spirit himself."

Carrie admitted she was intrigued, but she wouldn't willingly meet any man looking the way she did now. "Another time maybe."

"I'm having a party Friday night."

Carrie groaned inwardly and offered the oldest excuse in the world. "You know I hate those things. Besides, I don't have a thing to wear."

"Buy something."

For one crazy instant, Carrie actually considered it. At this time of the month she was traditionally low on ready cash but there were always her credit cards. Carrie made a quick decision.

It could be that Elizabeth was right about Shane. If he was everything her friend seemed to think, Camille's portrait wouldn't interest him. A free spirit who appreciated her art had to have some redeeming qualities.

But if Shane Reynolds bought the portrait, Carrie would know not to bother with him. But maybe, just maybe, for once in her life she could find a man who saw beyond the deceptive beauty of her sister.

"Well?" Elizabeth pressed.

"I don't know. Let me think about it."

"Don't take too long. A man like Shane Reynolds won't be single forever."

"I'll let you know."

"Do that."

The receptionist joined the two women and smiled cordially before handing Elizabeth a business card. "Mr. Reynolds is here for his appointment."

Elizabeth held Carrie's eyes. "You're sure you won't meet him?"

"Maybe Friday."

The older woman nodded. "As you wish. And, darling, do me a favor and check into buying a new car. I fear for your life in that . . . contraption." Elizabeth stopped abruptly. "By the way, do you have a title for the portrait?"

Unconsciously, Carrie nibbled on her bottom lip as she quickly decided. "How about *No Competition*?"

"Perfect." Elizabeth turned, prepared to meet her customer. "There aren't many women in the world who would want to compete against her."

"You're right about that," Carrie murmured.

Already Elizabeth's mouth had curved into a smile of greeting for her customer and Carrie doubted that her friend had heard her. She jumped down from the edge of the desk and drew in a steadying breath. Elizabeth had succeeded in arousing her curiosity. Shane Reynolds must be someone special to have Elizabeth singing his praises. Briefly she allowed a mental image to form in her mind. If beauty didn't impress him, it must be the result of some unattractive feature about himself. Men with imperfections were often willing to overlook the flaws in others. Perhaps he was short and balding. The thought served only to pique her curiosity. If he was inside an office all day, then he'd probably gone flabby. That sometimes happened to busy men who ate on the run and didn't take time to worry about proper nutrition.

Preparing to leave, Carrie's hand was on the doorknob when she gave in to the niggling inquisitiveness. If Shane Reynolds was standing in the other room, all she had to do was take a peek. No one would be the wiser.

Feeling a little like a cat burglar, Carrie opened the door and glanced through the crack. Tiny shock waves coursed through her body as her mental image went crashing to the floor. At first, all Carrie could see was a head full of gray hair. No, not gray but a fantastic shade of silver, as burnished as a new coin. Her thought was that he was older, possibly nearing middle age. But then he turned around, and her heart tripped out a staccato beat of surprised disbelief. The silver was premature. This wasn't some old, dignified architect, but a rawly virile man in his early thirties. One who was suntanned and vigorously provocative. The distinguished impression came from the sports jacket and dark pants that revealed discriminating good taste. The top two buttons of his shirt were unfastened to display hard, browned flesh. Carrie tried to tell herself he'd gotten that deep tan from a machine, but in her heart she knew she was wrong. This man hadn't the time for such vanity. He couldn't be termed classically handsome, but everything about him breathed overwhelming masculinity.

A curious ache grabbed her between the shoulder blades. Elizabeth was right. There was something about Shane Reynolds she liked. An awareness gripped her that was so strong her body went rigid. Rarely had the sight of a man affected her this way. It frightened her and, in the same heartbeat, exhilarated her beyond anything else in her twenty-seven years.

Attaining a grip on her emotions, Carrie turned and quietly slipped out the back door. She prayed fervently that Shane wouldn't buy the painting. If he appreciated the flagrant beauty in Camille, he would be like all the others. Desperately, Carrie hoped he wasn't. For once in her life, she wanted a man who could look beyond her glaring imperfections and discover the warm woman inside who was ready to burst out and be discovered. Her stomach churning with hope and expectation, she headed toward her station wagon.

Thirty minutes later when Carrie pulled into her driveway, her hands felt clammy. Her small, one bedroom cottage sat on a cliff high above the rolling Pacific Ocean. The price had been outrageous. It was ironic that the one great love of her life would be a narrow strip of rocky beach and not a man. Camille collected the men while Carrie boldly etched her emotions across bare canvas, revealing the innermost secret places of her heart.

She breathed in the fresh clean scent of the ocean and experienced an unshakable freedom. Someday she'd like to build a bigger home, but for now the cottage suited her perfectly.

Smiling to herself, Carrie unlocked the front door and thoughtlessly tossed her purse aside. She paced the living room once, then moved directly to the phone in the kitchen and punched out a number with an impatience she rarely experienced.

"Dove Gallery," came the soft voice of the receptionist.

"This is Carrie Lockett for Elizabeth Brandon," she breathed out, swallowing down her uncertainty. From the minute she left the gallery she hadn't stopped thinking about Shane. Already she'd made a decision.

"Could you hold the line a minute?"

"Yes."

"Darling," Elizabeth answered a moment later. "It's that car, isn't it? You've had an accident."

"Of course not," she laughed, and added without preamble, "Did he buy the painting?"

"Shane Reynolds?"

Who else did Elizabeth think she was referring to, Carrie mused with a hint of irritation. "Yes, Shane Reynolds."

"He was impressed with it. In fact, *No Competition* has been the center of interest all afternoon."

Her lashes fluttered down with distress. "But did he buy it?"

Carrie heard Elizabeth's sigh. "I'm afraid you're going to be disappointed, but he didn't. I felt sure he would. Do you need the money? I could probably—"

"No . . . no," she gasped, too happy to think about something as mundane as food or house payments or anything else. Her voice was remarkably even when she spoke. "Don't worry about me. And Elizabeth, about that party Friday night—count me in. I'd enjoy coming."

"What a pleasant surprise. Shane will be there. I'll introduce you, if you like."

"I'd like that very much." Already she felt hope stirring within her breast. It had been a lot of years since she'd experienced this much expectation.

"I'll see you Friday at seven then."

"At seven," Carrie repeated and after a cordial farewell, she replaced the telephone receiver.

She shouldn't feel this excited. She was setting herself up for a big disappointment and behaving like an adolescent. Carrie didn't care. A surge of exhilarated expectancy washed through her. Something wonderful was about to happen. She could feel it all the way to the marrow of her bones.

Although she hadn't eaten since early morning, Carrie wasn't hungry. But past experience dictated that she fix herself some dinner or she would be out of sorts later. Warming up a can of tomato soup and popping half an English muffin in the toaster, she hummed cheerfully as she worked in the cozy kitchen.

The front door clicked open and Carrie glanced up to see her twin sister saunter into the house.

"Hi." Camille was dressed in a pale pink sundress that showed off the ivory perfection of her bare shoulders. "Something smells good."

"Tomato soup. Do you want some?"

"No thanks. Bob's taking me to dinner later."

"You've been seeing quite a bit of him lately, haven't you?" Camille had been dating Bob for a couple of months. Perhaps Camille was feeling that the time had come to start thinking about marriage and a family. Naturally, Camille would marry first.

"Bob's all right." She helped herself to an apple from the basket on the kitchen table. "He's rich, you know."

"I didn't." But knowing Camille, money wouldn't necessarily enhance a man's attraction. For that matter, it didn't mean all that much to Carrie, either. The two of them were so different outwardly, but shockingly alike in other ways.

"He's in exports," Camille elaborated.

"That's interesting." For the moment, the only thing that concerned Carrie was why the toaster was taking so long to produce a crisp muffin.

"I think he might ask me to marry him." She said it as though the idea of marriage utterly bored her. She sat on the oak chair with the webbed seating and crossed her long, shapely legs.

Caught off guard by the disinterested announcement, Carrie turned to face her sister. "Will you accept?"

"I don't know. Bob's really nice, but if I'm going to settle down there are certain things I want in a man."

"Oh?" Carrie was surprised. She didn't think her sister had given the matter of what she wanted in a marriage partner anything more than a fleeting consideration. "What qualities are you looking for?" Carrie's own wants were specific. She wanted a husband who would be her best friend, her shock absorber and, in some ways, her compass.

"I'm not sure." Camille bit into the apple. A tiny drop of juice ran down her chin and she lazily wiped it away. "Money isn't all that important. It's nice, I suppose, but there are so many other qualities I want in a husband."

"Maybe it's time you started thinking about it."

"He should want a family," Camille said thoughtfully.

"I want a husband with integrity and tenderness," Carrie added.

"But I don't think he should be overly fond of children."

"Why not?" Carrie couldn't understand her sister's thinking on that one.

"I only want one child," Camille explained.

The soup started to boil and Carrie removed it from the burner. "Why only one?"

"Babies fluster me. You're the motherly type. Not me."

Maybe that was because Carrie had taken over the role so early in life. Their mother had died unexpectedly when they were twelve and Carrie had assumed many of the duties around the house. Their father worked a lot of overtime and the two were often left to their own devices. First thing after school, Carrie started the evening meal while Camille did homework. For Carrie, studying was a breeze. On the other hand, Camille had a difficult time studying. She often lamented her inability to "remember things the way Carrie does." Consequently it was Carrie who cooked, cleaned and struggled to maintain a balance for everything else in a young girl's life.

"I took your portrait into Dove Gallery today."

Camille didn't look surprised. "I imagine someone will buy it quickly." She said it with absolute certainty, but Carrie wasn't sure if this was a back-handed compliment to the work she'd done on the portrait or if Camille felt few could resist her beauty.

"It's already causing some stir." The exaggeration was only slight. Elizabeth would have it sold by the end of the week and Camille's flawless beauty would be intriguing men for years to come. Few would give a moment's thought to the artist, and actually Carrie preferred it that way. Camille belonged in the spotlight while she was strictly background material.

"You're a good artist, Carrie."

Her twin's compliment came as a complete surprise. "Thank you. But usually it's the subject that will cause a painting to sell."

A small smile revealed Camille's perfect white teeth. "Are you telling me the subject of this last painting of yours will help it to sell?"

"Undoubtedly."

"Good." Camille took another bite of the apple, pleased with herself.

The English muffin popped up from the toaster and Carrie reached for it, piling tuna fish over the top and placing a sliced tomato over that. She carried her meal to the table and sat down opposite Camille.

"I'm happy to hear the painting will sell soon."

Carrie spread a paper napkin across her lap. This was the second time her sister had alluded to money. "Is there something you needed?"

Camille straightened and cocked her head to one side. "I was wondering if you could float me a loan. You know I'll pay you back."

Carrie knew her sister would, but borrowing money to hold her over until pay day was becoming increasingly common. Camille's job as a beauty consultant for a large downtown store paid well. Unfortunately, Camille had never learned to budget. Things were tight this month for Carrie as well and she was hoping to buy a new dress for Elizabeth's party. "I suppose I could loan you some, but not much." Carrie had been rescuing Camille from the time their mother died and old habits die hard.

"You don't sound that eager," Camille returned. "You know how I struggle to make ends meet."

"We all do." She stood and reached for her purse, and handed Camille a fifty dollar bill, which left her with loose change in the bottom of her purse.

"Thanks." An irresistible smile lit up Camille's baby blue eyes. "I'll talk to you later." Already she was on her way out the front door.

"Right. Later." With a grumble, Carrie returned to her soup. It happened every time. Camille asked and Carrie gave, without so much as batting an eyelash.

That night Carrie dreamed that Shane Reynolds was walking along the beach with her. The salty breeze buffeted against them as their feet made deep indentations in the wet sand. Shane slipped a casual arm around her shoulders and smiled into her eyes with a love so strong that it would span a lifetime. In the morning, Carrie woke feeling warm and wonderful. And a bit foolish. She wasn't a young girl to be swayed by romantic dreams, nor did she waste her time on fantasies. She was a woman with a woman's heart. And for the first time in months, she felt the longing for a man who would share her life.

Sitting up, she looped her arms around her knees and rested her chin on top of the thick blankets. She was determined to attend Elizabeth's party Friday night and meet Shane Reynolds. The first hurdle had already been passed. He'd seen Camille's sleek elegance and hadn't been lured by all that untarnished beauty. Elizabeth had claimed he wouldn't be, but experience had taught Carrie otherwise.

Her first order of the day was to shop. After spending a fruitless morning downtown, Carrie found the dress in a small boutique tucked away from the mainstream of the large downtown shopping complexes. The pale green dress was the most expensive thing she'd ever owned. The smooth silk whispered over her skin and clung in all the right places, giving an illusion of beauty. Wearing this dress and standing in the right light, Carrie felt that someone might be able to detect the fact that Camille was her sister.

The color did something fantastic for her eyes. No longer did they resemble dirty swamp water. Unexpectedly, there were flashes of jade and a touch of emerald in her usually pale, nondescript eyes. The dress was definitely worth the price, Carrie reasoned, signing the charge slip.

On Friday evening she arrived at Elizabeth's party feeling light-headed and a little nervous. Her stomach felt as if she'd been on a roller coaster all afternoon, pitching and heaving with every turn. She'd been extra careful with her makeup and pinned her hair away from her face. Her mother's pearls graced her slender neck and ears. Normally she avoided the mirror, but this evening Carrie had stood in front of one so long she was half tempted to ask it who was the fairest in the land. But Carrie already knew the answer. Tonight she was going to give Camille a run for her money.

Carrie's smile was feeble when the maid answered the door and took her lace shawl and beaded purse. Her pulse soared at the sound of laughter, tinkling ice and a hum of conversation that drowned out the piano player.

Her eyes scanned the crowded room, seeking only one person and experiencing keen disappointment when she couldn't locate Shane Reynolds. It was still early and he probably hadn't arrived yet. People were everywhere, sipping champagne and chatting easily, but Carrie had never been good at making small talk. The roller coaster dipped and she placed a hand on her stomach to calm it.

From across the room, Elizabeth raised her hand in greeting and hurried to the door. "Carrie, darling, you're positively stunning."

"Don't look so surprised," she teased, her eyes gleaming. She knew she looked good. Her best. She wanted to make her meeting with Shane Reynolds a memorable one.

"But I am surprised," Elizabeth countered. "I've never seen you in a dress."

"I've been known to don one now and again."

"You should do it more often," she chastised lightly. "You're really very lovely."

The compliment was so sincere, Carrie blinked. Her first inclination was to make excuses for wearing the clothes she did. She quickly suppressed the idea, astonished at her own lack of self-confidence. Camille had always been the one for dresses. "Thank you."

"Now come, there are several people you must meet." Elizabeth made it sound as though the entire party had been waiting for Carrie's arrival as the guest of honor.

Elizabeth led Carrie across the room. Obediently, she followed, but her gaze skidded around the room, thinking perhaps she had merely missed finding Shane the first time.

Before she could make a thorough inspection, Elizabeth introduced Carrie to a long list of her most intimate and dearest friends. Many had bought Carrie's paintings, and she spent the next half hour answering questions and making what she hoped was stimulating conversation. A glass of champagne was handed to her. As she raised the glass to her lips, she spotted a flash of silver from across the room. The bubbly liquid stayed on her tongue as her eyes collided with Shane Reynolds's deep blue ones.

A slow, sensuous grin edged up the corners of his mouth and he slowly raised his glass in a silent salute.

The champagne stuck halfway down Carrie's throat. Tingling bubbles tickled the back of her tongue until she gulped the liquid down, nearly choking. Because she didn't know what else to do, she looked away. It had been years since any man had interested her as much as Shane Reynolds did. Cursing herself for her inability to flirt, she quickly looked back again. His smile was brilliant and directed solely at her. The palms of her hands felt clammy. The roller coaster unexpectedly left its tracks, plummeting downwards.

"You must meet Ashley Wallingford," Elizabeth was saying and Carrie returned her attention to another group.

Carrie felt Shane's gaze follow her. Drawn to him by a force stronger than any magnet, she sought him again. From across the width of the room, their gazes met and locked. This time he grinned boldly. She returned his smile and feeling extraordinarily fearless, Carrie winked.

"Carrie, have you met Ashley Wallingford?"

Her attention was quickly diverted to the other woman. "I don't believe I have," she returned, reluctantly pulling her gaze from Shane's. The first thing Carrie noticed about the elderly woman was her exquisite eyes. Deep blue, shrewd and perhaps a little calculating. This woman had lived a hard life and it showed in the network of wrinkles across her intelligent face.

"I understand you do portraits," Mrs. Wallingford asked conversationally.

"Some."

"Mrs. Wallingford was in this morning to see *No Competition*," Elizabeth added. "She was quite taken with it."

"You managed to portray an elegant, sometimes vain woman in a flattering light. I wonder if you always do as well."

Carrie sucked in her breath. "And I'm wondering if you're always so perceptive," she returned. Ashley Wallingford was a marvel.

"I try to be." A hint of amusement showed in those clear blue eyes.

Painting this woman would be a challenge and a treat. Already Carrie's fingers itched for a pencil.

"I would have purchased it," Mrs. Wallingford continued, "but unfortunately I was too late."

"It sold?" Carrie turned to Elizabeth.

Elizabeth's eyes brightened. "I thought you'd be pleased."

Mrs. Wallingford touched her arm. "I'd like to talk to you again, Carrie Lockett. You're an excellent artist. I'm hoping we can do business some day. Now if you'll excuse me?"

"Of course."

"Then I'll be getting in touch with you soon."

"I'll look forward to that."

As soon as the older woman had departed, Carrie turned her attention to the gallery owner.

"You're pleased about the portrait, aren't you?"

"Very. I didn't expect it to go so quickly."

"I was rather shocked myself. First thing this morning. I hadn't been open five minutes when..."

Carrie knew. In one horrible minute she knew. Her eyes darted across the room to Shane. The dream died as quickly as it had been conceived. And with it something young and vital shriveled up and wept inside of her.

"...when Shane Reynolds came into the gallery. He said he hadn't been able to stop thinking about the portrait all night. He didn't care about the price, he wanted it."

The fragile smile indenting Carrie's soft mouth cracked. "I see."

"I don't think you do," Elizabeth's soft lilting voice rose with excitement. "Not only is he crazy about the picture, he's dying to meet you."

Chapter Two

No," Carrie stated, shaking her head.

"What do you mean no?" Elizabeth's eyebrows shot up in surprise.

"I refuse to meet Shane Reynolds."

"But . . . why? Carrie, darling, are you feeling ill? You're quite pale."

"You're right, I'm not well. I shouldn't be here." She'd been a moron to entertain the idea that someone as handsome as Shane Reynolds would ever appreciate her. She swallowed her disappointment. She'd been an idealistic, romantic fool and worse, it hadn't been the first time.

"Carrie," Elizabeth gently placed a hand on Carrie's forearm.

"Thank you for inviting me," she said, backing away, taking a step with each word. "I'm sorry to leave so quickly."

"But Carrie, you just got here. Perhaps if you lie down a few minutes..."

"No...no." She bumped into someone and turned around sharply to apologize. "Please excuse me. I'm sorry, really sorry."

The couple looked at her as though seeing someone drop in from outer space. The floor pitched beneath her feet and Carrie inhaled a calming breath. Abruptly she headed for the front door.

Elizabeth followed, instructing the maid to bring Carrie her coat and purse. "I'll call you tomorrow," she said, looking concerned.

"Fine." She would have agreed to any terms as long as she could escape quickly.

"I'm sure once you're feeling better you'll reconsider meeting Shane."

There wasn't any possibility she'd change her mind, but she hadn't the strength to argue. The sooner she was out of there, the better.

It seemed an eternity before the maid returned with her shawl. Carrie wrapped it around her shoulders, gripping it as if an Arctic wind were raging against her backside. But the cold that ripped through her had nothing to do with the room temperature.

"You're sure you'll be all right?"

"Yes, yes." As soon as she left the party, she'd be a thousand percent better.

"Thank you for inviting me." Hurriedly she stepped out the door and rushed down the front steps. When she reached her car, she looked back to see Elizabeth standing in the open doorway, studying her with a concerned frown.

Carrie gave a brief wave and unlocked her car door. Her fingers trembled as she inserted the key into the ignition. Gripping the steering wheel, she pressed her forehead against the chilly plastic. Wouldn't she ever learn? What masochistic trait did she possess that refused to accept the most simple facts of life? There were no gallant princes riding around on white stallions ready to rescue her from her fate. From birth, she'd been doomed to stand in Camille's shadow. But she'd been compensated. She had her art. What more could she want?

Carrie released a jagged breath and started the engine. What more could she want? The list was so long it would take a lifetime to write it all down.

Once she was home, she stripped off the dress and hung it in the far reaches of her closet so she wouldn't be faced with it every time she opened the doors to choose a blouse. She wanted only to forget her hairbrained scheme.

By morning she felt much better. Her romantic heart had been wounded but she had an incredible recovery rate. The Shane Reynoldses of this world weren't meant for someone like her. The universe was full of too many beautiful women like Camille. Carrie had accepted that long ago.

Standing at the kitchen window, she watched the sea gulls swoop down to the beach far below. Carrie softly smiled and poured a cup of coffee, taking in the unspoiled beauty of the morning. White-capped waves crashed against the rocks and left a meandering path of foam across the virgin sand. A feeling of serenity crowded her heart.

Taking her coffee with her, she wandered down the steep trail that led to the beach. A few minutes of breathing fresh salty air would rejuvenate her.

The wind tugged at Carrie's unbound hair and whipped it across her face as she took the path to the beach. She found her favorite rock and sat, sipping her coffee. There was something so comforting about being on the beach. It didn't seem to matter what was troubling her; twenty minutes of watching the tide roll in made her feel like a new person, ready to take on the world and its problems.

Time lost meaning. A hundred chores demanded her attention at the house, but nothing was more pressing than her need to sit in the sun.

The sound of her name caused her to turn around. Her breath caught in her throat at the sight of Shane Reynolds's silver head. He was walking down the path, coming toward her.

He was the last person she expected to see and Carrie marched away from him, intent on escaping. She didn't want to see or talk to this man. He was trouble and she knew it.

"Carrie Lockett?"

She trudged on, ignoring him.

The sound of someone running after her caused her to quicken her pace.

"Ms. Lockett?" Shane was out of breath by the time he reached her side. Maybe it was a crazy idea to have come to her like this, but he hadn't been able to resist. Something had happened last night to make her run from the party and he wanted to know what.

"Yes?" She found it strange how immediately familiar his voice sounded. Cool and commanding, as though he expected an immediate response from her.

"You probably couldn't hear me."

Arms swinging at her side, she continued walking at a furious stride. "I heard you."

He swallowed down his irritation. "Then why didn't you stop?"

"Why didn't you get the message?" she demanded, struggling to present a facade of searing indifference. Now that she'd seen him up close, the illusion of virile maleness and overpowering masculinity was all the more pronounced. No wonder he'd purchased the portrait of Camille: he was breathtaking. A man as perfect as Shane would appreciate the extraordinary beauty of her twin sister.

"What's wrong?" His anger died at the look of hurt in her expressive eyes.

"Nothing," she lied, nearly breathless as she maintained her killing pace.

"I want to talk to you."

"And I'd prefer it if you didn't."

"Why not? I bought your painting. You're a fantastic artist and—"

"Listen," she said, whirling around, her hands on her hips. "You bought my painting. Big deal. I don't owe you anything. Who gave you the right to charge uninvited into my morning?"

His backbone stiffened. She wasn't anything like he'd expected or hoped. "Just a minute here, aren't you the same Carrie Lockett who sashayed into Elizabeth Brandon's party last evening and gave me a saucy wink?"

Oh heavens, Carrie had forgotten that. "I . . . had a twitch in my eye," she lied.

The robust sound of his laugh echoed around her. "You were blatantly flirting with me. You liked what you saw and said so. For that matter, I was intrigued too."

"I wasn't flirting." She continued walking, forcing him to jog to keep up with her.

"I want to know what made you suddenly change your opinion of me," he pressed. "All I really wanted to say was how much I appreciate your work."

"You've already told me that. Thank you, I'm grateful. Now you can leave."

He ignored that. "Elizabeth has mentioned you several times." He paused and struggled to maintain his control. He wanted to tell her that the only reason he'd attended Elizabeth's party was so he could meet her. But from her unfriendly stance, he could see that she'd refuse to believe that. "I assumed you wanted to meet me," he added.

"Then you assumed wrong." How easy it would be to fall for this man. One look and Carrie sensed danger. But if she was attracted to Shane then it would only be a matter of time before he discovered Camille. And it would be over even before it began. Her fragile heart couldn't afford to trust this man.

"Have lunch with me." The low-pitched request was a surprise.

"No."

Nonplussed by her refusal, he continued: "I don't know what I've done to offend you, but I'd like to make it right. Somehow we got started on the wrong foot."

"I'm simply not interested."

"Are you always this prickly?"

"Only with insufferable, arrogant men who bull-doze their way into my mornings."

The cutting quality of his dark eyes grew sharper as she struck a raw nerve. "I've been called a lot of things in my life, but never insufferable and arrogant."

"I trust my instincts." She had nothing more to judge him by.

"Then accept my apology for intruding, Ms. Lock-ett." His voice dripped with heavy sarcasm. Abruptly, he turned away and walked in the opposite direction. He didn't know what had happened, but he had too much pride to stand around and accept her insults.

Carrie paused as she watched him turn around and walk away. Her hands trembled and she sank onto the sandy beach, her lungs heaving. The wind made a frothy confusion with her hair and she let it blow around her face. Swallowing down the tightness that gripped her throat, she turned her concentration to the angry waves that pounded the beach. She hadn't wanted to be rude and prickly. It felt far more natural to smile up at him and share the beauty of this un-spoiled stretch of beach than to insult him. But it was better this way. Much better, yet far more difficult than anything she could remember.

With troubled thoughts, Carrie climbed the steep path back to the small beach house. She tried to con-vince her sagging self-confidence that she was saving herself a whole lot of heartache. Pausing on the back porch, she unceremoniously stuffed a pile of dirty clothes into the washing machine.

The phone rang just as she was adding the laundry soap. She reached for it automatically, stretching the long cord around the kitchen door, and held the receiver between her ear and her shoulder. "Carrie here."

"Darling, you survived."

"Elizabeth." Instantly, Carrie's fingers froze against the washer's dial. She regretted her panic from the night before. "I'm glad you phoned. I feel terrible about last night. I owe you an apology. My behavior was inexcusable."

"The only thing you owe me is an explanation."

"Yes, well, that could be a bit complicated."

Elizabeth wasn't about to be dissuaded. "I've got all day. I've known you a lot of years, and I've never seen you behave like that."

"But then maybe you don't really know me."

"Carrie, if you'd rather..."

"No, I'll explain." She owed Elizabeth that much. "I have a sister. I guess you can say that you've met her."

"Who is she, darling?"

From the tone of her voice, Carrie could tell that Elizabeth was searching through her memory. "As I recall, you found her intriguing..."

"The portrait?" Elizabeth was aghast. "The girl in the portrait is your sister?"

"My twin sister."

"Your twin sister," she repeated, obviously stunned. Her voice wobbled between two octaves as she struggled to disguise her shock.

"We're nothing alike, believe me."

"I can tell that, darling."

"Then you can also understand why I don't want to meet Shane Reynolds."

A short silence followed. "No, I can't say that I can."

"Elizabeth, think about it. Anyone who appreciates Camille's beauty isn't going to be interested in me. Good grief, people wouldn't even guess we came from the same family. Camille is everything I'm not."

"I thought I explained that Shane Reynolds isn't the type of man to be impressed with beauty."

"Right. That's why he bought the painting."

"He purchased that portrait because you painted it and for no other reason."

"I doubt it, Elizabeth, I sincerely doubt it."

Their conversation ended five minutes later, and with flint-hard resolve Carrie returned to her Saturday morning chores and refused to waste another second thinking about Shane Reynolds. But as the day wasted away, Carrie did think about him. She hadn't wanted to be rude. She hadn't wanted to push him away when everything in her yearned to reach out to him. Maybe Elizabeth was right and Shane was different. But she doubted it, knowing that once he met Camille it would all be over.

Her thoughts were still confused when the doorbell chimed the following afternoon. Carrie was washing her hands, wondering what she should eat for lunch. All morning she'd been sitting with paper and charcoal, sketching faces. Every one of them was Shane. Even the women and children had a strong resemblance to the silver fox who dominated her thoughts. Her floor was littered with the evidence of her frustration. Drying her hands on a rag, she hurried toward the door. Camille never bothered to knock so it wouldn't be her sister.

On the other side of the door, Shane shifted his weight from one foot to the other. He hadn't stopped thinking about this feisty little artist all night. She intrigued him. Outwardly she was as prickly as a cactus, but her work revealed a warm, loving soul on the inside. There was obviously something about him she didn't like. Fine, he'd find out what it was and take it from there.

Smiling, Carrie unlatched the lock. "Hello." The welcome faded from her eyes as her gaze met Shane Reynolds. Her heart throbbed at the unexpectedness of seeing him a second time and she glanced guiltily over her shoulder, thinking that the charcoal sketches had materialized before her eyes. He'd come back and, after her rudeness on the beach the day before, she couldn't imagine why.

"Hello." His gaze softened.

Gathering her resolve, she opened her mouth to tell him to leave, but the command in his eyes stopped her.

"Listen, I don't know what was wrong before, but I'd like to talk this out."

"I—"

"Before you argue with me, let me assure you that I'm really quite a pleasant fellow. And if you'll listen I'd like to make a confession."

"What kind of confession?"

"I knew who you were long before Elizabeth's party."

"But how..."

"You were at the gallery about a month ago and I saw you leave. Elizabeth pointed you out to me." Remembering the gentle woman that afternoon told him something was wrong. That woman and the one on the beach weren't the same person.

Carrie remembered the day. It was one of those rare San Francisco days when the sun was shining and everything in and about the world was perfect.

"I followed you to Fisherman's Wharf," he continued. "And watched you buy a bright red balloon."

"I didn't get it for me." That was only a small white lie.

"I know. I saw you give it to the little girl, but not until after you'd carried it with you for several blocks."

"I was looking for a *special* little girl." One like herself, plain and unassuming, someone who didn't command the attention of others. A child who walked in the shadow of an attractive brother or sister.

"Then you caught the cable car and—"

"You were spying on me."

"Actually, I was trying to come up with an original way of introducing myself," he admitted with a chagrined smile. "I'd just figured out that the straightforward approach would be best when you jumped on the cable car. I didn't make it."

"Oh." How incredibly inane that sounded.

"Now that I've bared my soul, I'm hoping that you'll share a picnic lunch with me." Surprise showed in her eyes and Shane knew that half the battle had been won. At least she was speaking to him.

Carrie had to put a stop to the way her heart reacted to this man. "It looks like rain." Any excuse would do.

"There isn't a cloud in sight," Shane said, contradicting her.

"I don't have anything to pack for lunch."

"I do," Shane ventured again. "I figured if you wouldn't go out to lunch with me then I'd bring it to you."

"You're very sure of yourself." Her resolve managed one last rally.

"I'm very sure of what I want," he responded with a breath-taking smile that was meant to melt her defenses. He succeeded.

"And what exactly do you want?"

"To get to know you."

"Why?" Carrie asked, lacing her fingers together. He really was something.

"That's the part that confuses me." A frown marred the urbane quality of his handsome features. He was unsure of his feelings. He didn't usually get much resistance from women. He was successful, wealthy, and reasonably attractive. Women gravitated toward him. After their minor confrontation on the beach, Shane had thought his attraction could be attributed to the challenge Carrie represented. Today he knew differently. He'd wanted to meet her for weeks. There was a reason she'd responded to him the way she had. And Shane was determined to find out why.

"I . . . don't know.' Carrie hesitated, knowing that she'd already lost the inner battle.

"Come on, Carrie, I'm not really all that bad."

With a growing sense of anticipation, she smiled and with a nod asked, "Can we haul it down to the beach?"

"I was hoping you'd suggest that."

She followed him out to his car where he retrieved a small wicker basket and blanket. She still couldn't believe that he'd come back after she'd been so rude and unreasonable. Carrie realized she shouldn't be so glad, but she was. A warning light went off in her head like a traffic light gone berserk, but Carrie chose to ignore it, cursing her foolish heart for wanting this so badly.

Leading the way down the well-worn path to the beach, Carrie commented, "It's a beautiful day, isn't it?"

Shane's warm gaze held hers. "Yes, it is."

A mere smile from this man could charm snakes. Surely he possessed more enchantment than her meager defenses could easily fend off. Her stomach knotted in a tight ball of nerves as she determined that she wouldn't let one picnic with him influence her feelings. No matter how difficult it was, she'd remain coolly detached. She must!

Her smile was wavering by the time they reached the sand.

"This is perfect," Shane commented when she paused to spread out a blanket. Behind his lazy regard, Carrie felt that he was watching her every move. She struggled to remain unaffected.

"We don't often see bright sunshine so early in the summer." The lag in conversation was unsettling. Why was Carrie talking to him as though he were a tourist? Anyone who lived in San Francisco knew what the weather was like.

Shane didn't comment, almost enjoying her obvious discomfort. "The weather's generally pleasant this time of year."

Silently, Carrie wished he wasn't so damned logical. Surely he could recognize that she was making an effort to be polite. She owed him that much. Women wouldn't often ignore a man like Shane Reynolds. Unfortunately, the knowledge served only to heighten Carrie's awareness of him and his many charms.

"Maybe we should eat now," he suggested.

"Sure," Carrie agreed eagerly.

Shane handed her napkins and pried the top from the bucket of chicken. They ate in silence.

By the time they'd finished, Carrie was wondering why she'd ever agreed to this.

Stretching his long legs out in front of him, Shane crossed them at the ankles and rested his weight on the palms of his hands. "Do you feel like talking now?"

"I suppose." Carrie made busy work, picking up the litter. Her gaze avoided his.

"What happened the other morning?" Once he passed that hurdle he could venture onto Elizabeth's party.

"When you said you wanted to talk, I assumed you meant about the painting."

"Not particularly." His blue eyes smoldered as they studied her.

"Then why'd you come here?"

"I wanted to get to know you."

"I don't understand why." Carrie's voice trembled.

"Elizabeth told me what a rare talent you are." Shane knew she'd feel more comfortable discussing her art.

"You don't look like the type of man who goes around forcing yourself on artists."

"You're right, I'm not. Something happened the night of the party for you to have run away almost immediately after you arrived. I want to know what."

"You're imagining things." If she'd known this was going to turn into an interrogation, she would never have agreed to this picnic.

"Maybe I was imagining something at the party," he reasoned. "But Saturday morning you were rude and abrupt."

"Why did you come back then?"

"I felt given time, you'd change your mind."

His confidence grated on Carrie. "You've got a big head."

"Agreed, but in the past it's worked to my advantage."

"Okay, you've met me. Now what?" She wasn't up to playing verbal games with him. The sooner she discovered why he was so curious about her, the sooner she could deal with her emotions.

"I'm intrigued."

"Don't be. What you see is what you get." She held out a thick strand of rusty colored hair and batted her long lashes at him.

His deep husky laugh floated with the wind. "But I like what I see."

"Then you need bifocals." He wouldn't have bought the painting of Camille if he appreciated someone like her. "Why did you buy the portrait?" she asked bluntly, needing to know.

He smiled lazily and his handsome features looked years younger. He didn't know what it was about that painting that disturbed her and he weighed his words carefully, not wanting to reveal the true reason just yet. "If you want the truth, I needed something for my office. I was hoping a few of the matchmakers would view the woman as my current love interest."

"*No Competition* should do the trick." This was even worse than she'd realized. A feeling of disappointment burned through her.

"Who is she?"

It took Carrie a moment to realize Shane was asking about Camille. "A beautiful woman." Her answer was clipped and cool.

"Yes, she's that, but the portrait isn't the first of your work that I've seen."

"Oh?" Elizabeth had already told her Shane had purchased other of her works.

"I have one of your seascapes and a couple of your earlier watercolors."

"Oh." Her vocabulary had unexpectedly been reduced to words of one syllable.

"You're very good."

"Thanks."

"It's to the point where Elizabeth contacts me the moment you bring in something new."

"I'm flattered."

"The problem is that lately I haven't been able to separate the paintings from the artist."

Startled green met intense blue eyes and Carrie caught her breath before it jammed her throat. If he saw her personally in her work, then he must glimpse her insecurities and all her glaring faults.

"I feel like I already know you, Miss Carrie Lockett."

Her heart was threatening to pound right out of her chest.

"I look at your painting of spring flowers blowing free in the wind and I sense your love of nature and generosity of spirit. You love with an intensity that few seldom see or experience."

Tight-lipped, Carrie lowered her gaze. Every word he said was distinctly unsettling. He'd blown her up in his mind to be something she wasn't. "I'm not Mother Theresa."

"The seascape taught me that. There's depth to you. You're an anchor while others are sails. I also sense rebellion and perhaps a hint of jealousy."

Shane Reynolds unnerved her, and Carrie struggled to cover her confusion by responding sharply without thought to what she was saying. "Who wouldn't be jealous? You bought the painting, so you obviously appreciate beauty."

Her words echoed around her like taunts and Carrie closed her eyes to a lifetime of being second best.

"Is that why you called it *No Competition*?" he asked quietly.

"Of course," she came back flippantly.

"But there's no comparison between you and the woman in the painting."

"Exactly." Coming to an awkward stand, she brushed the grains of sand from the back of her legs. She hoped to hide her confusion by taking a walk along the beach.

Shane followed. "Do you always walk away when the conversation doesn't suit you?"

"Always." The tension she struggled so hard to disguise threaded its way through her nerves. "Listen, I appreciate the compliment. Any artist would. But you've met me and now you can see that I'm nothing like you imagined."

"But you are," he interrupted. "And a whole lot more."

"Sorry, wrong girl."

"Correction, right woman." He slipped his hands into his pant pockets. "I want to get to know you better."

"I'm all out of résumés. Check with Elizabeth."

"I don't want to read about you. Let me take you to dinner."

"No." She hated this, and silently pleaded with him to leave things as they were.

"Why not?"

"Do I have to spell it out for you, Mr. Reynolds? Thanks, but no thanks. I'm simply not interested."

"I don't believe that."

"Have you got such a colossal ego that you believe no woman can turn you down?"

"Maybe so. I'm not giving up on you, Carrie."

"Please." Her voice softened and her green eyes pleaded with him. "I hate being so rude. I'm simply not interested."

"Give it some thought," he coaxed gently.

"There's nothing to think about." She wanted to cry. "Believe me, I'm flattered, but the answer is no. Pure and simple. N-O. No."

He struggled not to argue with her. He'd come up with some other way to reach her. "You can't blame a guy for trying."

"No, I don't blame you." She looked out to the sea to avoid his smoldering gaze. "Thank you for the lunch." And everything else, she mused, wondering what it would mean to her life to send him away.

He didn't pursue her curt dismissal, but cocked his head slightly and without a word turned and walked away.

Shane was the type of man of whom dreams are made, and she was turning him away. But it was more than the fact he'd bought Camille's picture that prompted her to do so. Shane frightened her in a way that was completely unfamiliar to her.

Monday afternoon the curiosity got the best of her, so Carrie contacted Elizabeth Brandon at the gallery.

"Carrie, darling, it's good to hear from you."

Carrie drew in a deep breath. "Why didn't you tell me about Shane Reynolds?"

"But, darling, I did."

"All this time he's been buying my paintings."

"I already mentioned that."

"I know, but you claim lots of customers ask for my work."

"You're becoming appreciated."

"But Shane Reynolds is different."

"How's that?" The soft lilt of Elizabeth's voice indicated that she was enjoying their conversation.

"He's the kind of man women follow around drooling over."

Elizabeth gave a tiny laugh. "A customer's physical attributes have little to do with his appreciation of the arts."

"That's not what I meant." The problem was Carrie didn't know what she meant.

"Listen, darling, I'm glad you phoned. I was about to contact you. The president of Little & Little called this morning, hoping I could get in touch with you about doing his portrait."

Smiling, Carrie decided she was wasting so much time worrying about Shane Reynolds, she was neglecting her business. If she didn't get another commission soon she'd go crazy. Today even the seascape she was painting had shades of Shane Reynolds's eyes in it. "I'm interested."

"I thought you might be. He wants you to come to his home for the initial interview. Have you got a pen?"

"Yes." Carrie pulled out a piece of paper. "Go ahead."

Elizabeth gave her an address in the Nob Hill area. "Can you make it soon?"

"Whenever he likes."

"Is tomorrow evening convenient?"

There wasn't any reason she couldn't make it. It wasn't like she had a busy social calendar. Tomorrow would be like any other night of the week. She'd cook a TV dinner and immerse herself in a good book. "Sure, I can make it."

"Wonderful. I'll send over the usual contract."

The following evening at the appointed time, Carrie pulled up in front of the address Elizabeth had given her. She tucked her sketch pad under her arm, and swung her purse strap over her shoulder as she looked both ways before crossing the street.

The bell chimed once and Carrie prepared a ready smile. These early interviews could be the most important. The smile died, however, when Shane Reynolds opened the door.

A grin slashed his handsome features. "I wondered how long it would take you to get here."

Chapter Three

Y ou?'' Carrie cried, managing to keep her anger at a low simmer. Shane had tricked her and used Elizabeth in his schemes. Carrie was so furious she could hardly speak.

"I see you're right on time." His smile was warm enough to melt a glacial ice cap as he casually leaned against the door jamb and crossed his arms.

Carrie refused to be trapped in his sensuous web and fumed at the amused curl of his mouth. "You think you're clever, don't you?"

"I try to be." If the truth be known, Shane wasn't all that pleased with the underhanded methods he'd used to get Carrie to his home. Once again he'd spent a sleepless night wondering why her reactions to him were so cold. After their meeting on the beach, she'd represented a challenge. Now it was more than that. She was a spirited, intriguing woman and those wide green eyes spitting fire at him melted his determination to forget her.

Stepping inside the house, Carrie discovered a wide entryway tiled in opulent marble. A winding staircase veered off to the left, and to her immediate right double doors opened into a large, old-fashioned parlor. At any other time, Carrie would have appreciated the character and personality of the house, but under the present circumstances, she couldn't see beyond Shane's deception.

"I suppose I owe you another apology," he began, but Carrie quickly cut him off.

"Do you always go to such drastic measures when a woman refuses you?" Her voice was hard and flat. She pressed the sketch book so tightly against her chest that her fingers lost feeling. "I don't appreciate this."

"I didn't imagine you would. But I wanted to talk to you."

"We talked yesterday." Carrie couldn't take her eyes off him. His sports jacket was unbuttoned, the front held open by a hand thrust in his pocket. Her pounding pulse told her she was flattered that he'd gone to all this trouble to see her again, but her head insisted that so few women turned Shane Reynolds down his oversized ego was on the line.

"We may have talked. But I didn't get to say all the things I wanted," he countered. Although he struck a casual pose, Carrie was aware that he was every bit as alert as she.

"If I sit down and listen, will you promise to leave me alone?"

He mulled over her words. "I don't know if I can verbalize everything."

"Then the deal's off." She pivoted sharply and marched out the door. No footsteps sounded behind her as she crossed the street to her car. Her emotions were in an upheaval. She was running like a frightened child from the things she wanted most in life. She *was* scared. The attraction she felt toward Shane was so strong she had to fight against it with every breath. It would be so much easier if he hadn't bought the painting of Camille. She might have been able to rationalize the situation then.

A turn of the ignition key resulted in a low grinding sound. Carrie stared at the gauges in disbelief, hoping they could tell her something. Her car might be old, but it had always been faithful. Again she tried to start the engine. This time the grinding sound was lower and sicker.

Tossing a curious glance out her side window, she noted Shane standing on his front porch watching her. He was smiling as though he had the world by the tail. She returned his taunting grin, thinking he was the most infuriating man she'd ever known.

She climbed out of the car and walked around the front to open the hood, chancing a look in Shane's direction. He'd come down the steps and was standing under a lovely maple tree on the other side of the street.

Carrie felt her hateful freckles flashing like neon lights, she was so flustered. Not knowing what to do, she touched a couple of gadgets as though she were a faith healer. Then feeling like a complete idiot, she climbed in the front seat again and turned the key.

Nothing.

"Did I ever tell you I am a whiz with mechanical things?" Shane asked, enjoying this unexpected turn of events.

"No," she grumbled under her breath. The least he could do was offer to help. He didn't volunteer and Carrie refused to ask.

"I'm quite good," he continued. "From the time I was a child there wasn't anything I couldn't take apart and put back together again. Including a car engine."

"How interesting," Carrie returned sarcastically, getting out of the car.

"I'm certain we could come up with a small compromise." He advanced a step.

"Exactly what kind of compromise?" She glared at him, her hands on her hips.

"Dinner in exchange for the magical touch of these mechanically tuned fingers." He held up his right hand and flexed his fingers.

"I was thinking more along the lines of a quarter for the use of your phone." She held her shoulders stiff.

"Carrie, Carrie, Carrie," he said her name mockingly. "Am I such an ogre? Is the thought of dinner with me so unappealing?"

She longed to shout that any meal shared with him would be divine. It wasn't him she didn't trust, but herself. It would be far too easy to fall for this man.

"If you want my word that I won't touch you," he added, "then you have it." But he gave it grudgingly.

"That's not it," she murmured miserably.

"Then what is?"

She arched her shoulders and tears brimmed in the murky depths of her eyes. "What—what do you want with someone like me? I'm not the least bit attractive and you're... well, you're one of the beautiful people of this world. I'm so ordinary."

Shane's smiling expression was gone. Vanished. He couldn't believe what he was hearing. Not attractive. Good heavens, where had she gotten that impression? She was magnificent. Spirited. Talented. Intelligent. He crossed the street in giant strides and paused to stand in front of her. His brow creased in thick lines as his frown deepened. "Not attractive? Who told you that? You're perfectly wonderful and I defy anyone to say otherwise."

"Oh stop," she cried and wiped the moisture from her face, more furious with herself than Shane. Tears were the last thing she'd expected. She could believe him if he hadn't bought Camille's portrait.

His fingers began to lightly trace her face, starting at the base of her throat, stroking the triangle formed by the hollow. The thick pad of his thumb sensuously brushed her collar bone, the feel of his finger slightly abrasive against her soft, clean skin. Carrie swallowed convulsively as the muscles in her throat contracted. She couldn't breathe properly. His sandpaper touch was warm and gentle, reminding her of velvet. His words were just as smooth and she knew she couldn't trust either.

"I don't know you," she told him, her voice choked to a low, husky level. Her senses were whirling.

"And I feel like I've known you all my life."

"What do you want from me?"

"Time. When you get to know me better, you'll realize I don't give up easily. If I want something, I simply go after it."

"And for now you want me. But why?" Her knees shook under the intensity of his gaze. She fought off the sensation of weakness.

His hands cupping her shoulders, he tried to put his feelings into words. When he looked at her paintings he lost sight of the artwork, caught instead by the artist. "I'll never hurt you, Carrie. I promise you that."

Somehow she believed that he wouldn't intentionally hurt her. But already he had her senses spinning. He could easily pull her into his orbit and she would be lost. "If I have dinner with you, then will you help me with my car?"

"I'd help you even if you don't stay," he said with a roguish grin. "But I'd like it if you would."

"I . . . I am a little hungry."

The smile that lit up his eyes came all the way from his heart. "I was hoping you'd agree." His hand reached for hers, curling around her fingers. "I'm really an excellent cook."

Her guard slipped. It was so much easier to give in and smile at him than to struggle against the pull of her heart. "You cook, too. I doubt that there's much you don't do."

He laughed, and the vibrant sound echoed around her. "You do have a lot to learn about me, Carrie Lockett." He led her back inside the house and into the plush dining room. The table was set with long, tapered candles at each end, and a floral centerpiece dominated the middle.

"Do you eat like this all the time?" Carrie had assumed Shane was wealthy, but he didn't seem the type who would bother with formality at mealtime every night.

He looked almost boyish when his amused gaze met hers. "I wanted to impress you."

"You succeeded."

"Good."

But that wasn't the only thing he'd succeeded in doing. Against every inner battle she'd waged, Carrie lost. He held out the shieldback chair for her and once she was seated, he proceeded to bring out their meal.

As he claimed, Shane was an excellent gourmet cook. With her defenses down, Carrie chatted easily with him throughout the meal, telling him about art school and how she'd met Elizabeth and come to work with her.

"Ask me anything you want," he told her over dessert, pleased with how well their meal together had gone. "As far as you're concerned, my life is an open book."

Carrie took him at his word. "How old are you?"

He frowned slightly and touched the neatly trimmed hair, briefly worried that his premature gray disturbed her. "Younger than I appear—thirty-three."

"I think your hair makes you look distinguished." She didn't add devilishly handsome to the list. His ego was big enough already.

He smiled crookedly. "It's a family trait. My father was completely gray by age thirty. By the time I was in high school I already had a few gray strands. I beat out dad by two years."

Carrie found it amazing that he would be self-conscious of a trait that made him look so dignified and genteel.

"What about your tan? You didn't get that here." Certainly not in San Francisco in June, Carrie knew.

"I recently took a business trip to Tahiti."

"It's dirty work, but someone has to do it. Right?" she teased.

"Right. Now is there anything else that curious mind of yours wants to know?"

No need hedging around the subject. She longed to ask it and he was waiting. "Have you ever been married?"

"No."

"Why not?"

"A variety of reasons."

Carrie lowered her gaze to her strawberry torte. "Don't try to tell me there haven't been women."

"A few." He touched the corner of his mouth with his napkin. "During my college days I was too busy with my studies to be involved in a relationship. Later it was my career."

"And now?"

"And now," he repeated, looking directly at her, "it's time."

He said it so softly that Carrie felt like a popcorn ball had stuck in her throat. "Oh."

"Okay," he murmured. "My turn."

Carrie's eyes gazed into his. "What do you mean?"

"It's my turn to ask the questions."

"All right." But she wasn't eager.

"Married?"

"No," she said it with a small laugh.

"Why's that question so funny?"

She couldn't very well tell him that she could hardly be a married woman and feel the things she did sitting across the table from him. "No reason."

"How long have you been painting?"

She grinned, warming to the subject of her art. "Almost from the time I could remember. As a little girl I gave the letters of the alphabet faces and personalities. It took the first three years of grade school to learn to write without adding ears and mouths to each letter. Numbers were even more difficult."

"Numbers?" he frowned. "Why those?"

"It's hard to explain."

"Try me."

Somehow Carrie believed Shane would understand where others had failed, including her own father. "To me, each number has a color and a feeling. The number one is white and pure and ever so lonely. Two is pink and healthy. Seven is red and vibrant. Nine is black and foreboding."

"Why?"

Carrie shrugged one delicate shoulder. "I don't know. I've always thought of them that way. I gave up trying to reason it out." For that matter, so had her teachers.

"What about family?"

"I have one sister. What about you?" she asked, quickly steering the subject away from Camille.

"Three married sisters and a passel of nieces and nephews." His gaze shone with a curious light and it was impossible to look away.

Gazing at Shane with his eyes warm and electric, Carrie yearned for her pen and pad. He intrigued her. He'd make an excellent model; the planes and grooves of his face were just short of craggy and yet he was incredibly good looking. She longed to capture him on canvas with exactly the look he was giving her at that moment. Every facet of his features suggested strength of character and an elusive inner spirit.

"I'd like to paint you," she announced, unable to tear her gaze from his. "I don't know if you were serious when you contacted Elizabeth."

"I was serious." But only because having her paint him would give him an excuse to be with Carrie.

"Then you should know what you're letting yourself in for. I require ten sittings of a half-hour to an hour each."

"Fine. When can we start?"

Shane may readily agree to these sessions, but Carrie realized that sitting still was contrary to this man's personality. He was a doer, a go-getter, a human bulldozer. It wouldn't be easy for him to sit quietly for any length of time. He'd be a challenge, but already Carrie felt that a painting of Shane Reynolds could well be her best work. "I'd like to get a few preliminary sketches tonight."

"Fine."

As it turned out, Shane worked on her car while she sat on the grass and tried to capture his likeness. "You're not making this easy," she complained. His bulk was folded over the side of her out-dated station wagon so the only clear picture she had of him was from the rear. Quickly she penciled that. Laughing, she flipped the page and drew him in oily coveralls and a heavy beard.

"What's so amusing?" His voice echoed from under the hood.

"Nothing," she replied absently as her hands flew deftly over the page. "But I don't think I dare show you what I'm drawing."

"Instead of picking on me," he instructed, "draw yourself."

Carrie did, depicting herself as a giraffe with long, wobbly legs and knobby knees. Thick, sooty lashes framed round eyes and her hair fell in an unruly mass of tight curls around her face. Her freckles became the giraffe's spots. "Here, for your collection," she said and tore off the sheet, handing it to him.

Amused, Shane wiped his hands clean with a white handkerchief before taking the page. But the smile in his eyes quickly disappeared as he viewed her self-image. "You see yourself like this?"

"Of course." Her own good humor vanished. The eyes that had been so warm and gentle hardened as he glared at her, intimidating her with an anger barely held in check.

"You can't argue with the hair," she added hurriedly. "It's just as thick and unruly as in the picture." To prove her point she webbed her fingers through the glorious length, holding it out from her head. "The freckles are also beyond debate. You can't overlook them. And the knees, well, you've only seen me in a dress once so..."

She didn't finish as Shane crumpled the portrait in a tight ball, destroying it. "Don't poke fun at yourself, Carrie. There's no reason."

"It...was only a little joke."

"At your own expense. I don't like it."

"Well tough toast, fellow." She didn't like the emotions he was bringing out in her. She wasn't Camille, and she'd been compared to her sister all her life—always coming in a poor second. Camille was the beauty and Carrie...well, Carrie had her art.

His eyes seemed to burn straight through her. Carrie shuffled her feet uneasily. "The car's fixed?"

"You shouldn't have any problem with it now." Almost instantly he regretted his heated response to her sketch.

"I hate to eat and run, but I'd better think about heading home."

Shane didn't argue and Carrie awkwardly moved to the driver's side of the car. "Thank you for your help. I truly appreciate it. And the dinner was excellent. You're right about being a good cook. No wonder you never married." Realizing how dreadful that sounded, she gulped and added, "That's not to say that you'd marry someone because she was a good cook. You're not that kind of man." Wanting to make a hasty retreat, she opened the car door and slid inside. "Nor would you marry a woman because she had money," she babbled on, furious with herself for not stopping. "Since you're wealthy yourself and all. What I mean..." Carrie felt her freckles flash on like fluorescent light bulbs. "You just aren't the type of man to do that sort of thing."

Resisting the urge to laugh, Shane closed her door, his hands resting on the roof of the car. "You seem to have marriage on your mind. Is this a proposal?"

Carrie nearly swallowed her tongue. "Good grief no. It's just that...oh dear." Before she said anything more to regret, she fumbled with her keys, wanting only to escape further humiliation.

"Carrie." He said her name so softly that she jerked her head around.

A finger under her chin closed her gaping mouth. Her sensitive nerve endings vibrated with the contact.

Slowly, his head bent toward hers, his warm breath stirring the wispy hairs at her temple. Tripping wildly, her heart pounded against her ribs as she realized he was going to kiss her.

With unhurried ease, Shane claimed her mouth, his lips playing softly over hers, tasting, caressing, nibbling. When he'd finished and straightened, Carrie gazed at him wide-eyed. Speaking, breathing, even blinking was impossible.

"I'm serious about the portrait," he murmured, stepping away from the car.

Mutely, Carrie nodded, lost and utterly confused. Fumbling with her key, she started the car and prepared to shift into drive.

"Carrie?"

She turned to him.

"You're not a giraffe, but a graceful, delicate swan who thinks of herself as an ugly duckling."

It was all she could manage just to pull away from the curb. The heat from her blush descended all the way down her neck. Like an idiot, she'd babbled on trying to cover one faux pas, but instead had created another and another until she'd made a complete fool of herself.

By the time she arrived at the beach house, Carrie was convinced she could never face Shane Reynolds again.

"Where were you the other night?" Camille asked, her lithe body folded over in the white wicker chair while Carrie painted.

Carrie did her utmost to concentrate on her current project, a still life. "With a client. How did your dinner date go with Bob?'' She preferred to stay away from the subject of Shane. Her sister was perceptive enough to recognize that Carrie's feelings toward him weren't ordinary. From past experience, Carrie knew better than to discuss any male friends with her sibling. More times than Carrie cared to count, Camille had stolen away her boy friends. The amazing part was that Camille hadn't even been trying. Men naturally preferred her to Carrie. Who wouldn't? Camille was beautiful.

If Camille did happen to learn about Shane, it could well be that her twin would find him as appealing as she did. Few men were strong enough to resist Camille's abundant charms.

"Bob fancies himself in love with me." Camille's dark head dipped as she ran the nail file down the length of her long nail.

"That's not unusual."

"No, I do seem to collect the admirers, don't I?"

She said it with such a complete lack of interest that Carrie had to fight to hide a smile.

"I don't know though," Camille continued, paying an inordinate amount of attention to her nail.

"Know about what?"

"About Bob."

"What's there to know? Either you love him or you don't." Almost immediately Carrie realized how uncaring that sounded. Camille had come to her with a dilemma and Carrie was being curt. "I didn't mean that the way it sounded."

"That's all right. Bob is my problem."

"But I'm your sister."

Camille offered her a weak smile. "There are lots of other fish in the sea. What I think I need is a break from Bob so I can do a little exploring."

"Maybe that's what we both need." But Carrie wasn't silly enough to let her sister know about Shane.

"You always could love better than me," Camille admitted with a half frown that only slightly marred her stunning good looks. "And yet the men always flocked to me and I'm the cold fish."

"Camille, you aren't." Her sister may have a few faults—who didn't? But Camille also possessed a wonderful

capacity to love. She just hadn't found the right man yet.

Camille arched two perfectly shaped brows as she gave the matter some consideration. "You'll laugh if I tell you that I think I may be half in love with Bob."

"I wouldn't laugh. In fact, I think it's wonderful."

"Is it?"

"I think so."

"He's got his faults."

"Camille," Carrie said and laughed aloud. "Everyone does."

Camille hesitated and concentrated on her fingernail. "I suppose. Now tell me about your new client. You're hiding something from me."

Returning her attention to the canvas, Carrie did her best to disguise her feelings. "What's there to tell? He wanted his portrait done, that's all."

"Come on, Carrie," Camille laughed, sounding like a kitten purring. "You're holding out on me."

"There's a sketch of him over there if you're interested." She pointed to the pad on the table top.

Camille reached for the drawing Carrie had done of Shane as a bearded man in coveralls. "He doesn't look like he can afford to have you paint his portrait."

"You're probably right," she hedged.

With her head cocked to one side, Camille continued to study the drawing. "He does have an interesting face though."

"If you like that type."

"I think I could get used to him. Did he give you the name of the garage where he works? My car's been acting up lately. I might have him look at it."

Carrie pinched her lips together in an effort to disguise her anxiety. For her to show the least amount of interest in Shane would be to invite Camille's curiosity. "He didn't say." Taking a gamble, she added. "But I have his address if you want it."

Tucking her nail file inside her purse, Camille shook her head. "Another time, perhaps."

The tension between Carrie's shoulder blades relaxed. "Whatever you say."

"I've got to go. Bob's meeting me later and I want to look good."

Camille couldn't do anything more to improve her already flawless appearance. It was difficult to polish perfection.

As soon as Camille was gone, Carrie reached for the phone. She'd delayed calling Shane all afternoon. Every time she thought of the things she'd said, the embarrassment went all the way to her bones.

"Hello." His greeting was brusque.

"This is Carrie Lockett. Is this a bad time?"

"Carrie." Her name was delivered with a rush of pleasure.

In her mind's eye, Carrie could picture him relaxing and leaning back to smile into the receiver. Her own pulse reacted madly and she pulled herself up straight. "I'm calling to set a schedule for your sittings. I'd like to begin tomorrow afternoon if possible." She felt the need to elaborate. "The first few sittings can be done anywhere. I can come to your house or your office, whichever you choose. Later it would be more convenient if you could come here."

"Either is fine. Let me check my schedule."

In the background, Carrie could hear him flipping pages. "How does four o'clock sound?"

"That'll be fine."

"Would you mind coming to my office?"

"Give me the address, and I'll be happy to."

"My, my don't we sound formal. Has the car given you any more trouble?"

"No . . . but I haven't been out today."

"The next time you're at the service station have the attendant check the carburetor."

"All right." She hesitated, not wanting the conversation to end. "I want you to know how much I appreciate your fixing it."

"And I'm grateful that you stayed and shared dinner with me," he added softly. "I'd be willing to do a complete engine overhaul if it meant you'd come again." The warmth in his tone was mildly disturbing. But then everything about Shane Reynolds disturbed Carrie.

"No thanks, perhaps another time."

"I'll hold you to that."

"I'm taking a class tonight."

"I'm pleased to know it isn't because you're seeing another man—or are you?"

"No." She didn't feel like admitting that he was the only man she'd dated in a month. Her 'dates' were more between friends than the result of any romantic interest.

"Good. What I know won't set me to wondering."

Carrie found it highly amusing that someone as handsome as Shane Reynolds would feel threatened by anyone she'd dated.

"I'll see you at four tomorrow," she told him.

"I'm looking forward to it."

Unfortunately so was Carrie. Far, far more than she should.

Wednesday afternoon, Carrie entered Shane's building a few minutes to four. She'd dressed in a blue linen jumpsuit, and tied her hair at the base of her neck with a silk scarf. A good portion of the early afternoon had been spent preparing for this meeting, but not in the way that Carrie usually readied for a painting. Instead, she sorted through her closets and spent extra time on her hair and makeup, all the while berating herself for the time and trouble.

"I'm Carrie Lockett," she told the receptionist. "I have a four o'clock appointment with Mr. Reynolds."

The attractive woman in her early twenties smiled at Carrie. "Mr. Reynolds mentioned you'd be coming. If you take a seat, he'll be with you in a moment." She punched a button on the phone line and picked up the receiver. "Ms. Lockett is here for her appointment."

Carrie took a seat and chose a magazine; she knew she'd probably have to wait a few minutes. Idly flipping through the crisp pages, she hadn't time to examine one issue before the door opened and Shane appeared. "I'm sorry to keep you waiting."

Slowly she came to a stand. "I've only been here a couple of minutes." They gazed at each other in a tender exchange.

"Come in, won't you?"

She would have willingly walked over hot coals to get to him. *You've got it bad, girl,* she mocked herself. "Thank you." She hoped her voice sounded cool and professional and knew she'd failed miserably.

"That'll be all for today, Carol," Shane told his secretary.

Carrie stepped inside his office and stopped cold. Camille's portrait hung on the wall opposite his desk in bold splendor, her dark-haired beauty dominating the room. Shane had told her the portrait hung in his office, but she'd forgotten. Abruptly she looked away, fighting the tightness in her breast. Every day Shane sat in this room and stared at the stimulating beauty of her sister. Each time he picked up the phone his gaze would rest naturally on Camille. As much as Carrie had tried to forget it, the fact remained that Shane found Camille beautiful. And if he stared at the creamy smooth perfection of her sister long enough, Shane couldn't help notice the flaws that stood out like giant fault lines in Carrie.

Shane motioned for her to take a seat. "Elizabeth sent over the contract," he said, holding out the paper to her.

"I hope you haven't signed it," she said in a low, tight voice. "Because I don't think things are going to work. I've given the matter some thought and decided that I wouldn't be the best one for this job. I'm sorry, Shane. Really sorry." She turned and fled from his office.

Chapter Four

Carrie—" Shane raced after her, ignoring the startled looks of his colleagues. He didn't know what was troubling her, but he wasn't about to let her run away from him a second time. He caught up with her outside the elevator. "What is the matter with you all of a sudden?"

"Nothing." She swallowed down another lie. "Really. I...just realized that I'm overextended timewise and...doing another portrait now would be too much for me." She couldn't tell Shane that it was impossible for her to work with him while he stared at Camille's perfect features. Carrie was likely to be placed in the position of having to respond to Shane's curiosity about the woman in the portrait. No one could look at Camille and not want to know her.

"I've got a signed contract," he reminded her, placing his hand on her shoulder in an effort to halt her progress. "We've agreed on the terms and I expect you to hold up your end of the bargain."

"Shane . . . I can't."

Curious bystanders were beginning to gather around them and Carrie was feeling more miserable by the minute.

"Let's get out of here," he mumbled, reaching for her limp hand. Instead of waiting for the elevator, he led her toward the stairwell. They hadn't gone more than a few steps when Shane turned to face her. "What is it with you? You have got to be the most unreasonable female I've ever known. You're hot, then cold. First the portrait's on, then it's off. You can't seem to make up your mind about anything."

"I'm sorry."

"Don't tell me that again."

"All right." From the way she behaved around him, Carrie considered it a wonder that he wanted anything to do with her. "If we mutually agree to tear up the contract—"

"No." His voice was both hard and flat. "I hired you to do my portrait." He wouldn't let her slip through his fingers that easily.

"But surely you understand that I can't."

"Why not?" he shot right back.

"Because . . ." How weak that sounded!

"Carrie, come on." He paused and pushed his fingers through his well groomed hair. "Let's get out of here. It's obvious we need to talk."

While they marched down the stairs, Carrie's mind frantically sought a feasible explanation and quickly came back blank. Nothing would satisfy Shane except the truth, and she wasn't willing to reveal that.

Once outside, Shane escorted her across the busy intersection into a nearby cocktail lounge. Carrie was grateful for the semi-darkness that shrouded the room. Her face felt hot with angry embarrassment. She was angry with herself and embarrassed that Shane wouldn't accept her feeble excuses.

They were no sooner seated when the waitress approached. Absently Shane ordered two glasses of wine and paid for the drinks when they arrived.

"All right, I'm listening," he coaxed. "Why do you want out of the contract?"

The smile that curved her lips felt as brittle as scorched parchment. Twirling the stem of the wineglass between her palms helped occupy her hands. "It isn't that I don't want to do your portrait."

"You could have fooled me," Shane muttered disparagingly.

"I think I'd do a good job."

"I *know* you would."

His confidence in her abilities produced a spark of genuine pleasure. "I . . . like you, Shane."

"I haven't made any secret about the way I feel about you. But you're like a giant puzzle to me . . ."

"And some of the pieces are missing," she finished for him.

He chuckled and relaxed, leaning against the back of the chair. His smile was slightly off center and devastating. "Exactly."

Carrie took a sip of her wine and felt the coiled tension drain from her arms and legs. She'd been looking forward to this meeting all day. Seeing Camille's portrait hanging in Shane's office had nearly ruined everything.

"Is there anything else you wanted to say?" Shane inquired, studying her.

"Yes." She paused and cleared her throat. She was anxious, yet aware of a tingling excitement deep inside her. It happened every time she was around Shane. He was the most special man she'd ever known. But she was afraid, so very fearful that once Camille learned about him, it would be all over. Since Shane found Camille's portrait so intriguing, Carrie doubted that he'd find the woman any less so.

"Can we start again?" she asked, her voice slightly strained and wobbling.

"I think we'd better." He stood and glanced around the room. His large hands folded over the top rung of the chair as he nodded curtly in her direction. "I hope I haven't kept you waiting, my dear." He spoke as though he'd only just arrived.

Carrie chuckled, and glanced at her wristwatch, playing his game. "Only a few minutes."

"I see you've ordered the wine." He sat and reached for the wineglass, tasting it. "My favorite. How did you know?"

"Lucky guess."

She resembled a frightened fawn and Shane couldn't understand it. "Now, about the portrait," he said conversationally.

Carrie stiffened. She couldn't help herself. "Which portrait?"

He didn't understand why there would be a question. "The one you've agreed to paint of me."

Visibly, she relaxed. "Ah, yes, that one."

"Shall we do the first sitting today?"

"Today?" She had everything with her. There wasn't any reason not to start with the preliminary sketches. "If you like."

"Of course." He stood and placed a handful of change on the table. "Are you ready?"

It took a minute for Carrie to realize that he wanted to return to his office. "You mean now?" She groped for a plausible reason not to go back there. Her mind was befuddled. Her wit deserted her. "Today? You mean today as in...now?"

"Yes." His arched brows formed an inquisitive frown. "Is that a problem?"

"Well, actually, I'm in a bit of a rush. I was thinking that since we're here...and your office is over there..." She pointed to the entrance of the lounge. "It seems a waste of time to travel all the way over there when we're..."

"Here."

"Right."

"Do you have something against my office?"

"Your office?" She swallowed uncomfortably. "Don't be silly. I've only been there once." As she spoke she reached for the sketching pad. "What could I possibly have against your office?"

"I don't even want to try guessing the answer to that one," he grumbled, downing the last of his wine.

Taking her thick-leaded pencil from her purse, Carrie angled the pad of paper in front of her and began sketching his bold features. Her fingers worked at a hectic pace, transmitting the image from her eye to the sheet. As soon as she completed one pose, she flipped the page and started on another, seeking the best possible way to catch the man and his personality.

She worked intently, unaware of the curious looks cast in their direction.

"When do I get to look?"

"Soon." The one word was clipped and short-tempered; her concentration was intense.

"Do you want me to hold my head a certain way?"

"What I want is for you to keep your mouth closed."

He snapped it shut, but she noted the way his lips quivered as he struggled to hold back a lopsided grin.

Finally, when she couldn't stand it another minute, she rested the pad against the edge of the round table. "All right, what's so blasted amusing?"

"You."

"Me? Why?"

"Explaining it would be impossible. But I'll have you know that I'm revealing my strength of character here."

"How's that?"

"I doubt that few men would demonstrate so much restraint."

Restraint. The man was speaking in riddles. "How's that?"

"Kissing you seems to be my natural inclination."

Shock paralyzed her hand. Her palm sagged against the paper until the pencil slipped from her fingers and dropped unceremoniously to the floor. Quickly she retrieved it, her cheeks flaming with hot color.

Smiling boldly, Shane's gaze captured hers. "You heard me right."

"But the room's full of people."

"It's dark in here," he countered, giving her a grin best described as Cheshire smug. "As I was saying, I'm showing a lot of self-restraint."

"Should I tell you how grateful I am?"

"It would help."

She finished the last sketch and handed the pad to him. "Then thank you, my dear Mr. Reynolds."

His eyes studied the likeness she'd drawn of him. "Nice."

"Is there one you prefer more than the others?"

"No. You decide." He wasn't especially interested in her doing his portrait. It was all a ruse, an excuse to get to know her better and learn what he could about this complicated woman.

"I will then."

"How about dinner?" His invitation cut into her thoughts. She was trying to decide the best angle to capture the force of his personality.

"Pardon?"

"You know—dinner—the meal which is eaten at the end of the day, usually after a long afternoon at the office. And most often after the time when a man has had a chance to relax with a glass of fine white wine."

"Oh, you mean *dinner*."

"Right." He gave her an odd look. "How about it?"

"Yes, I usually eat that meal."

He chuckled. "Since it seems that time of day, and we've already relaxed with a glass of excellent wine, how about sharing dinner?"

He offered the invitation with such charm that Carrie doubted if she could have refused him anything. He had to be the most patient man in the world.

Anyone else would have considered her a prime candidate for the loony bin.

"What kind of...dinner?" Still Carrie hesitated. The shop that employed Camille wasn't more than a mile from Shane's office, and if they chose a restaurant close by, there would be the possibility they'd run into Camille. Although they didn't look the least bit alike, the way Carrie and Camille shared thoughts was sometimes uncanny. Only last month, they'd celebrated their father's birthday and discovered that they'd each purchased him the identical golf shirt and birthday card. At other times, Carrie would be thinking about Camille and go to call her only to have Camille ring first, claiming Carrie had been on her mind.

"What kind of dinner?" Shane repeated the question with a perplexed look that was becoming all too familiar. "I was considering food."

"A popular choice. However, I was thinking more along ethnic lines. You know...Italian, Mexican, Chinese."

"You decide."

Carrie didn't hesitate. "Chinese." Camille had never been especially fond of vegetables and soy sauce. She leaned more toward a variety of expensive seafood dishes. For that matter, so did Carrie.

"Fine," Shane commented dryly, displaying little enthusiasm.

"You don't seem elated with my choice." He was the one who'd suggested that she choose.

He shrugged. "I was in Chinatown for lunch today."

"It doesn't matter to me," Carrie lied. "You decide." Her fingers trembled slightly as she sipped the last of her wine.

"Do you like seafood?"

Carrie released an inward groan. She should have known he'd suggest that. "Seafood?" Her voice echoed his.

Shane shot her a brief, mocking glance. "Yes. You know, fish, lobster, crab. That sort of thing. I've heard Billy's on the Wharf is excellent."

"I suppose that's fine." She dropped her gaze to the table, not wanting him to know how distressed she was. Camille had often raved about the food at Billy's.

"Mexican?" he offered next.

Instantly she brightened. "Great choice."

He mumbled something under his breath and shook his head. After he stood up, he said, "Let's get out of here before you change your mind."

She found it amazing that he wanted to have dinner with her after going through all that. She reached for her pad and purse. "I'm not going to change my mind."

A smile twitched at the corners of his hard mouth. "I won't believe it until I see it."

Shane held the lounge door open for her and they stepped outside into the bright sunshine. Side by side they walked along the crowded sidewalk. Rush hour traffic filled the streets. His hand came up to rest on her backbone just above her waist. Its guiding pressure was light, but enough for her to be aware of the contact and be unnerved by it. But then everything about this man seemed to affect her.

They were halfway down the block when Carrie caught a glimpse of a teal-blue Dodge convertible that resembled the model Camille drove. Rather than take a chance of being seen with Shane, Carrie made a sharp right hand turn and headed into the nearest store.

She had disappeared before Shane realized it. She was there one minute and gone the next. Stunned, Shane did a complete three hundred and sixty degree turn. He was utterly perplexed.

"Carrie." Shane whirled around again, attempting to locate her.

The car passed without incident. Carrie was so busy hiding that she didn't notice if it was Camille's car or not. Quickly she moved back outside. "Sorry, I...saw something on sale that I've been wanting." She flicked her wrist toward the black leather bedroom outfit complete with handcuffs and chains displayed prominently from the window. Carrie's shocked eyes went from the display window to the name of the establishment which made it abundantly clear as to their specialty.

Sucking in a horrified breath, she instantly turned fifteen shades of red. "Then, of course, I realized that I was in the wrong store. It was...some...other store."

"Naturally."

They caught a taxi at the next corner and Shane gave the man the name of a restaurant not far from Billy's on Fisherman's Wharf. After what had happened earlier, Carrie wasn't about to comment that this restaurant was too close to the one Camille frequented.

Their meal was delicious. Or, it would have been if Carrie had taken more than a token taste. Her appetite had vanished with the toll of her minor subterfuge.

After dinner, they took a short stroll around the waterfront, stopping in a few shops along the way. The whole time Carrie was conscious that it would be just her luck to run into Camille. They caught a taxi at the waterfront, and Shane escorted Carrie back to her station wagon.

"Thank you for dinner." She stood with her back to the driver's door. Her hands gripped the handle from behind.

"You're most welcome." Shadows darkened his face. The streetlight illuminated the area, creating a soft romantic atmosphere.

Carrie wished the lights were dimmer. She wanted Shane to kiss her and doubted that he would in such a well-lit spot.

She could feel him watching her as she spoke. "I had a nice time."

"Good. Maybe we can do it again soon."

She shrugged in an effort to disguise how pleased she was that he asked. "Sure. There are lots of good restaurants in Daly City."

"Daly City! What's the matter with downtown?" The things she said were so ridiculous they should be documented!

"Nothing."

His throaty chuckle did little to ease her discomfort. For the entire evening, she'd made one outrageous statement after another. This wasn't going to work. As badly as she wanted to be with Shane, trying to keep Camille a secret was far too complicated. She wasn't talented enough to pull off another night like this one.

His hand rested on the slope of her shoulders as his gaze caressed her. "Carrie, I want you to answer a question."

Danger alarms rang in her ears. Her instincts told her to avoid this at any cost, but she couldn't. Nor would she continue to lie. "A question? Sure."

"Not a difficult one." His hands slid from the curve of her shoulder up to her neck in a gentle caress. "Are you married?"

She relaxed and boldly smiled up at him while gently shaking her head. "No."

"You're sure?"

"Positive."

The only thing that could justify her behavior was if she had a husband or jealous boyfriend. His mind was afloat with questions. "Have you ever been married?"

"Never." So he assumed she was hiding from a man. She was so relieved she almost forgot herself and kissed him.

His hand molded itself to the gentle incline of her neck, his long fingers sliding into the silky length of her hair. "I want you to know how pleased I am to know that."

"At the moment, I'm rather pleased about it myself." But not for the reasons he assumed.

"I want to kiss you."

"I know." She wanted it too.

His mouth made an unhurried descent to her waiting lips. It seemed a lifetime before his mouth covered hers, his touch firm and blessedly warm. The moment their lips met, the tension of anticipation eased from Carrie and she responded by raising her arms and wrapping them around his strong neck.

The pressure of the kiss ended, but he didn't raise his mouth more than a hair's space. "I've wanted to do that from the moment I saw you this afternoon."

"You did?" All she could remember was him staring at the portrait of Camille.

He kissed her again. "After the wild goose chase you've led me on, you can't doubt it." His hands moved up and down her spine, arching her closer to his male length. "I'll see you soon?"

"Dinner?"

"If you like, but I was thinking more about the portrait."

Good grief, her memory deserted her the minute she was in his arms. "Naturally. I think I'd prefer it if we met at your house . . . or you can come to mine." But the latter was dangerous on the off chance Camille showed up, which she often did. "Your place I think."

"Fine."

"Friday?"

She blinked, trying to remember what day this was. "Okay."

He kissed her again and the pressure at the back of her neck lifted her on her tiptoes. Her hands explored his jaw and the column of his throat, her fingers finally settling on his shoulders.

"Friday then," he said as he breathed into her hair. Reluctantly, he broke contact. "Will you be all right driving out to your place?"

"Of course."

"I could follow you, if you'd like."

And probably not plan to leave until morning the way he was looking at her. "I'll be fine," she insisted. "Thanks anyway."

His hand covered his eyes. Good grief, blurting out the wrong thing must be contagious. "I didn't mean that the way it sounded. It's just that I usually escort my dates home. It doesn't feel right to let go of you here."

For once Carrie felt in control. She received immense pleasure at the look of consternation that tightened his face. "Are you saying you don't find me attractive?"

"You've got to know otherwise." Keeping his mouth shut seemed to be the best thing. He reached for her again, but she easily sidestepped his arms.

"You get an A for effort." Unable to resist, she tucked a strand of silver hair behind his ear and lightly pressed her lips over his. "I'll see you Friday. Seven?"

"Fine." He opened the car door for her and stepped back as she climbed inside.

She offered him a tremulous smile. Her mouth still held the throbbing heat of his kisses.

The drive home was completed almost mechanically. Briefly, Carrie wondered if Camille had seen her with Shane and what her sister would say if she had. Carrie wouldn't be able to hide him forever. Perhaps if she subtly approached the subject of Shane, it might work.

It wasn't until the following Thursday that Carrie had the opportunity to do exactly that. Camille stopped at the beach house to repay the loan, tucking the fifty dollar bill under the salt shaker on the kitchen table.

Carrie washed her hands and made busy work in the kitchen, trying to come up with a tactful way of addressing the delicate subject of Shane.

She didn't get the chance before Camille brought it up on her own. "I thought I saw you the other day."

"Oh?" Carrie froze.

"You didn't happen to have dinner near Fisherman's Wharf this week did you?"

Pretending to be distracted by slicing a lemon for the tall glasses of iced tea, Carrie shook her head. "I can't say it wasn't me." No doubt the double negative would confuse her twin.

"Were you alone?" Camille pressed, surprising Carrie.

"I went with a friend."

"Male or female?"

"Honest, Camille, what is this? The Inquisition?"

"I'm just trying to keep tabs on you. You're my only sister, for heaven's sake."

"What were you doing there?" The best way to handle this, Carrie felt, was to raise a few questions of her own.

"Bob and I went to Billy's."

Carrie delivered the ice-filled glasses to the kitchen table. "The last time we were here you said something about being in love with Bob. How did you know that you were even that much in love with him?" Oh dear, she was going to make a mess of this.

"So you *were* with a man," Camille cried with girlish delight. "I knew it. And obviously one you're wild about. All right, Carrie, give."

"You answer me first!"

"You mean about falling for Bob? I wish I knew. I like being with him. He's fun. But my whole life wouldn't depend on seeing him again. But then I think how much I'd miss him. As you can tell, I'm a tad bit confused."

"Do you think about him?" Carrie's thoughts had been dominated by Shane almost from the moment she snuck a peek at him in the gallery.

Camille shook the soft brunette curls of her perfectly styled hair. "I wish it were that easy. Whole days go by when I don't think about Bob. Well, he isn't completely out of mind. I don't know how to explain it." She studied her sister. "Are you in love?"

Carrie snickered. She couldn't help it. "With whom? It isn't like I've got scores of admirers just waiting for me to fall into their arms. Who would be interested in me when you're around?"

"It's not like I try to steal your male friends away. Half the time I don't even date them." Camille stated the problem in a nutshell. She wasn't attracted to them, but they sure were to her. Shane would be, too, once he met Camille. "Come on Carrie, tell me about him."

"There's no one," she insisted, taking a long swallow of the iced tea.

Camille cocked her head to one side as though viewing her sister for the first time. "You know I'd confide in you."

Carrie turned around. There had been plenty of times over the years when she'd resented her twin. Camille had it all. At least what everyone could see. Few cared that Carrie had a sharp brain and a God-given artistic ability. Men in particular didn't see past the exterior.

The phone pealed and Carrie stared at it as if it were a burglar alarm blaring out of control.

"Aren't you going to answer it?" Camille asked.

"Yes." She made a show of drying her hands before reaching for the telephone receiver. "Hello."

Her worst fears were realized the instant Shane spoke.

"Hello, Carrie."

She didn't dare say his name. "Hello," she said stiffly, holding her back rigid.

Shane hesitated, apparently sensitive to the reserved tone of her voice. "Am I catching you at a bad time?"

Ever since their evening together, she'd been hoping to hear from him. "Sort of," she admitted with some reluctance.

"Shall I call back a little later?"

"I could phone you." Her eyes looked anywhere except at Camille.

"I'm at the office. Do you have that number?" Shane asked.

"Yes. I'll call you there." She'd find some way to get rid of her sister. For once she was going to hold on to a man and she didn't care what tactics she was forced to use. Shane was the best thing that had happened to her in years.

"I suppose that was your handsome mechanic," Camille said when Carrie disconnected the line.

"My what?" Carrie was genuinely baffled until she remembered how Camille had assumed that Shane worked on cars.

"Remember you showed me your drawing of him the other day? You aren't going to be able to keep me from meeting him much longer, sister dearest," Camille insisted. "Don't you think I know what you're doing? You never have been able to keep anything from me for long. Good grief, every time you lie, your freckles become fluorescent."

Carrie's hand flew to her nose. "That's not true." Even as she spoke, she knew it was.

"And right now your nose alone could light up the entire Golden Gate Bridge."

"Oh, stop it, Camille. There is no one special in my life at the moment."

"And the Pope isn't Catholic."

"Camille."

"All right, all right. I'll meet him sooner or later. You won't be able to hide him from me forever."

The words were like an unwelcome bell tolling in Carrie's bemused mind.

"No doubt you're dying for me to leave so you can phone your phantom 'friend.' Well, I won't delay your conversation any further." Camille deposited her empty glass in the sink. "I just wish you were a little more open about this man."

"Why?" Carrie asked with a trace of bitterness. "So you can steal him away from me?"

"So there *is* someone." The delicate laugh that followed produced a shiver that ran up and down Carrie's backbone. "I don't think you have anything to worry about. Our tastes in men have never meshed."

That was true. Silently, Carrie watched as Camille waved and sauntered out the door. As far as men were concerned, beauty outdid talent and brains any day of the week. And Carrie was only beginning to believe that Shane might be the exception.

Playing it safe, Carrie waited an extra ten minutes after Camille left before anxiously reaching for the phone.

Carrie fussed all day Friday, more nervous about this one sitting than a hundred others. This was Shane she was going to meet. Shane, the man who had withstood her rebuffs, her craziness, and her complete lack of self-confidence and liked her anyway. As she dabbed expensive French perfume behind her ears and at the pulse points of her wrists, she imagined how calm and collected she'd be when they met. An eager smile curved the edges of her mouth. Shane wouldn't know her. Every time they'd been together, her behavior had been highly questionable. The man was a priceless wonder to have stuck things out with her. This evening she'd shock the socks right off him with her calm, cool reason. Tonight she had nothing to hide and no secrets to keep. She was there to paint his portrait and afterward Shane had insisted she stay for dinner.

Grabbing a bottle of an excellent California Chardonnay, Carrie was on her way. She'd looked forward to this night. Everything was going to be perfect.

The drive went smoothly and she was right on time when she pulled up in front of his elegant home.

Shane answered the door with a welcoming smile and rewarded her taste in wine with a light kiss across her surprised mouth.

"I thought we'd work in here tonight, if you don't mind." He led the way into his library.

"Sure," Carrie agreed, following him inside. It wasn't until she was completely inside the room that she noticed the portrait.

He had moved it. No longer was Camille's image hanging from the walls of his office. Shane had brought it home.

Chapter Five

Shane watched the expression of shock work its way across Carrie's pale features. She stood in front of the portrait and studied it as though seeing it for the first time and being astonished at her findings. Shane wished he could read her thoughts. It was obvious to him now that it was the painting that greatly distressed Carrie. Yet, he couldn't imagine why.

"You brought it here," she said in a tone that was so low it wobbled. "Why?"

"Is there a reason I shouldn't?" He moved around the desk and claimed the chair, hoping that his actions seemed nonchalant.

Carrie's attention drifted from Camille's flirtatious smile back to Shane. Taking his cue, she sat in the comfortable leather chair and set her supplies on the Oriental carpet.

"She's lovely." Again Shane's gaze rested on the painting.

Carrie ignored him as she took out the equipment she'd be using for this session.

"Don't you agree?" he pressed.

Carrie's stomach bunched into a painful knot as she answered him with an abrupt shake of her head. The tingling numbness that had attacked her throat soon spread to her arms and legs, leaving them feeling useless.

"There aren't many women that lovely."

Carrie clenched her jaw so tightly her molars ached. From the beginning she'd known how difficult it would be to stand in Camille's shadow. She'd so desperately wanted Shane to be different that she'd purposely ignored all the signs.

Holding her head high and proud, she boldly met his gaze. "She's probably one of the loveliest women you'll ever meet."

"I take it you know her personally?"

Carrie's fingers curled around the chair arm, her long nails denting the soft leather. "Yes, I know her."

His eyes surveyed the portrait with incredible tenderness. "She's fantastic."

"Yes." With a frantic need to be done with this assignment as quickly as possible, Carrie began the preliminary sketch.

"She's—"

"Don't talk," Carrie barked. Her hands flew over the page, softening the blunt lines of his craggy features only slightly as she worked.

Silent now, Shane relaxed against the back of the chair, crossing his legs and planting his hands on top

of his bent knee. His gaze drifted from the portrait to
Carrie, then back again. Slowly an amused grin appeared. Carrie had thought to fool him, but he had
figured it out. She'd done an excellent job on the portrait, but he'd seen through the guise. *No Competition* had to be a portrait of the artist.

Viewing it now, Shane understood why the portrait
intimidated Carrie, and he wished he could change
that. He was an architect and his profession had
taught him long ago that the outside was only a facade. Often alluring and appealing to the eye, but
useless as anything more than a front. It was the inside that mattered. Carrie Lockett was a woman of
grit. He realized that old fashioned word didn't fit the
image of this modern woman. In his mind's eye,
Shane envisaged Carrie as she might have lived a
hundred years ago. She was the pioneer type. One who
would set out to tame a wild land. A woman of sub-
stance who settled the farm lands and built the heart
of a new country.

Had she lived in those times, she probably wouldn't
have been given the opportunity to paint as she did
now. Her artistic talent would have been utilized in
different ways. Perhaps in the craft of quilting. The
genius of such work was only now beginning to be
recognized. His thoughts drifted to his own grand-
mother and mother, and he wished that they were alive
so they could meet Carrie. Both would have loved her.

Fifteen minutes passed without either saying a
word. Carrie's concentration centered on her work.
She'd captured Shane's likeness well, but it wasn't the
way she saw him. A photographer would do as well
and cost far less. Furious that she cared so much, she

viciously jerked the huge sheet off the pad and wadded it into a tight ball.

"Carrie..."

Rising to a stand, she angrily met his gaze. "Do you want to meet her?"

"Who?"

"Who else?" She waved her hand at the portrait, determined to get this over with as quickly and painlessly as possible. Once he met Camille he could have the woman he really wanted. Camille claimed that their tastes in men didn't mesh. This time her sister was dead wrong. Shane was Camille's type. Handsome, secure, talented. Everything her sister wanted and a whole lot more. But Camille wouldn't recognize his gentleness, his intelligence or his quick wit. But none of that mattered now. Shane wanted Camille and had from the very first. The adoring looks he'd been giving the portrait from the minute Carrie had entered his den proved as much. Unable to disguise his eagerness, Shane would be enthralled to meet her twin.

"Meet her?" Once again she'd managed to perplex him. "What are you talking about?"

Rarely had a man been more obtuse. "The woman in the portrait will be at my house tomorrow evening at seven. Be there."

A long moment passed before Shane responded. "If you insist."

The soft sound of his chuckle infuriated her and she glared at him with a lifetime of resentment burning in her murky green eyes. "It's what you want, isn't it? What you've wanted from the beginning? The artist was only the means of meeting the model. Fine. I just wish you would have been up front with me from the beginning.''

Before he could move around the desk, she'd picked up her briefcase and was marching out the den and toward the front door. "Carrie, would you kindly stop and listen to me?''

"No. Just be there.''

He chuckled again. "I wouldn't miss this for the world.''

"I didn't think you would.''

He followed her down the front steps. "Do you want to schedule the next session now?''

"No.''

"But I want you to continue the portrait.''

Carrie hesitated. "I doubt that you'll feel that way after tomorrow.''

"Don't count on it, Carrie.''

Holding the handle of her briefcase as though it were a lifeline to sanity, she sadly shook her head. "We can wait until tomorrow night and discuss it then.''

She had that hurt look about her again, and Shane yearned to reach out and hold her. From experience he knew she wouldn't let him when she was in this mood. Some day she'd come to trust him enough, but until then he had to learn to be patient.

"I'm not going to change my mind about the portrait or about you,'' he told her.

"Time will tell.'' One look at Camille and Shane would willingly forget her and the portrait he'd hired her to paint. Why shouldn't he when he had the real thing? As she had a hundred times in the past, Carrie would subtly drift into the background while Camille took the forefront. Only this time it hurt more.

From the front steps, Shane escorted Carrie to her parked car. He patted the hood and absently ran his hand over the faded paint of her outdated station wagon. He lingered while she climbed inside and inserted the key into the ignition.

"Have you had a mechanic look at it yet?" he asked.

"No. The man at the gas station told me to bring it in next week." She shifted the gears into reverse and waited for Shane to step back.

He did so grudgingly. He didn't want her to go, but couldn't think of an excuse for her to stay. It wasn't until she pulled onto the street that he remembered their dinner warming in the oven.

Carrie's heart was so heavy she felt as though a ton of bricks were pressing against her breast, her mind and her soul. She shouldn't blame Camille for her beauty, but this time she did. And even though the last person she wanted to speak to at the minute was Camille, she forced herself to call her sister and be done with it as quickly as possible.

Once back at the beach house, Carrie didn't feel the comfort and welcome she usually did. Shadows lurked in the corners. Even the ocean below looked gray and depressing.

She didn't bother to turn on the lights and fumbled around in the dark, dropping her equipment as she came through the front door. She curled up on the sofa, wrapping her arms around her knees and pressing her chin in her collarbone.

There was no help for this. It had to be done. Gathering her resolve, she moved into the kitchen and lifted the phone. She hesitated an instant before punching out the number that was as familiar as her own.

"Hello." Camille's soft voice was fuzzy as though she'd been sleeping.

"Camille, it's Carrie. Is this a bad time?"

A short, surprised silence followed. Carrie seldom contacted her sister. Camille was the one who came to her with a multitude of problems and questions. Carrie was the mother; Camille the child. Only this time their roles were reversed. Camille would solve the problem that burned through Carrie like a slow fire.

"Carrie, what are you doing phoning this late? Is anything wrong?"

"No... not really."

"You don't sound right."

Carrie didn't doubt that. She felt terrible—on the verge of being physically ill. "I know," she said and her voice dropped almost to a whisper. "Can you stop by tomorrow night say around seven, seven-thirty?"

"Why?"

Carrie backed against the kitchen counter and lifted the heavy hair off her forehead as her eyes dropped closed. "There's someone I want you to meet. Someone who wants to meet you."

"I don't suppose it's a man?" Camille was joking, seeming to enjoy this and noting none of the pain that had crept into Carrie's voice.

"Yes, a man, a special one I know you'll like."

"So you've decided to unveil your mechanic friend." The statement was followed by a low, knowing laugh.

"He isn't a mechanic. Shane's an architect. He's the man in the sketches you saw."

Camille hesitated. "He did have an interesting face."

"Yes." That was all Carrie would admit about Shane.

"Aren't you afraid I'll try to steal him away?"

Carrie bit unmercifully into the corner of her bottom lip. That wouldn't be necessary. Shane had never been hers. Their whole relationship had been built around the woman in the portrait. And that was Camille.

"I wouldn't, you know," her twin added, more serious now.

"He's yours if you want him," Carrie said with as little emotion as possible. "He's interested in you already."

"That's amazing, since I've never met him."

Carrie felt she might as well let the bomb drop now as tomorrow night. "He's the one who bought your painting."

"Really." A small excited sound came over the wire. "How extraordinary. And now he wants to meet me? I'm flattered."

"I knew you would be." A muscle leaped in her tightly clenched jaw and she uttered the statement with a faintly sarcastic tone.

"He must be wealthy if he could afford one of your paintings."

"I thought money didn't interest you." Jealousy seethed through her veins. She'd fought the battle so often and conquered it so readily that the ferocity with which it raged now shocked her. "I'm sorry to cut this short, but we'll have time to talk tomorrow night."

"I wouldn't miss this for the world." Camille sounded like a schoolgirl promised a trip to the circus. She hesitated for an instant. "You're sure you don't mind, you know, if Shane and I go out? You seemed quite taken with him the other day."

"Mind?" Carrie forced a laugh. "Why should I mind?" Why indeed, she repeated as she severed the phone connection. Why indeed.

The following day, Carrie left the answering machine on to pick up any phone calls. There wasn't a single person she felt like talking to and anyone important would leave a message. By lunchtime she counted six calls. Playing back the recorder she discovered that Shane had phoned four times. The first time he told her that he was sorry to miss her and that he'd check back with her later. The second call revealed a hint of impatience. Again he claimed he'd catch her later. On the third call, he said that he knew she was there and purposely not talking to him. If he didn't have to attend an important meeting he'd drive out and prove it. The last call was to apologize for his anger on the third call and tell her that he'd see her that evening. They'd get this mess straightened out once and for all.

Carrie listened to each message with a hint of impatience. She didn't know why Shane thought there was a mess. For the first time since she'd learned he'd bought *No Competition*, everything was crystal clear.

At six she showered and dressed, choosing her best linen pants and a pale silk blouse. No doubt Camille would arrive resembling a fashion queen. Carrie had no desire to further emphasize the contrast.

Using oyster shell combs, she pulled her thick hair away from her oval face and applied a fresh layer of makeup. The doorbell chimed when she'd finished spreading a layer of lipstick across her bottom lip. She smoothed out the color on her way to the front door. Knowing Camille, she would be so eager to meet the man who had purchased her painting that she'd probably decided to arrive early.

She forced herself to appear welcoming as she pulled open the door.

"Hi," Shane said. "I know I'm early, but I couldn't wait any longer."

The shock of seeing him momentarily robbed Carrie of her ability to talk.

"Did you get my phone messages?" He came into the cottage and paced the area in front of her sofa.

Carrie clasped her hands together and shook her head. "I got them."

"But you didn't bother to return the call."

Personally, she couldn't see any reason she should. Seeing him again was difficult enough. "No."

"This has gone on long enough."

"What has?" He was angry, but it was pointed inwardly as though he was furious with himself.

"This whole business with the portrait."

She squared her shoulders. "I couldn't agree with you more."

"I know." He reached out and gently laid his hands on the ivory slope of her shoulders.

"What do you know?" Now she was the one in the dark.

"About the painting."

"Would you kindly stop talking in riddles?"

"I admit to being fooled in the beginning. The coloring was tricky and the changes in the features were subtle ones. That's the reason I didn't buy *No Competition* the afternoon I first saw it."

Carrie stared at him in wide-eyed expectation. "What are you saying?"

"I'm on to you," he said with a small, tight laugh. "*No Competition* is a self-portrait."

Carrie was too stunned to respond.

"You took all the beauty stored inside that warm, loving heart of yours and painted it on the outside. Only—" He paused to position his thumb against her trembling chin. "Only, you did yourself an injustice. Your beauty far surpasses the loveliness of the woman in the painting. Your brand of attractiveness is much more captivating than any surface beauty."

"Shane..." Shimmering tears filled her eyes. She couldn't believe what he was saying. No one had ever thought she was attractive. And certainly never lovely. Not when compared to Camille.

"If you recall, I didn't buy the painting that first day. If the truth be known, I was disappointed in it."

"But—"

The pressure of his finger against her chin stopped her. "The portrait disturbed me until I realized what you'd done. I'd followed you that day on Fisherman's Wharf and witnessed for myself the real Carrie

Lockett. I don't need anything more than you, Carrie. Exactly as you are this moment."

"Oh, Shane." She blinked in an effort to restrain the ever-ready flow of emotion. "Don't say things like that to me. I'm not used to it. I don't know how to react."

"I was drawn to you the first time I saw you and your appeal grows stronger with every meeting."

Carrie stared at him with disbelief mingled with awe, unable to tell him how much his words meant to her flagging self-esteem.

"I don't need the beautiful woman in the portrait," he told her gently. "Not when the real woman in flesh and blood is right here."

Her brow knit in concentration. "You mean that, don't you?"

"With everything that's in me."

The realization that Camille—the real woman in the portrait—was about to descend on them at any second, vaulted Carrie into action. "In that case, I'll let you take me to dinner."

"I was hoping you'd agree to that." He didn't seem to hear the urgency in her voice and walked around the coffee table to take a seat on the sofa.

Not wanting to reveal how important it was that they leave soon, Carrie reached for a light jacket and draped it over her shoulders. "Shall we go to Billy's?" she asked, edging toward the front door.

"How about a glass of wine first?"

"I took my last bottle to you the other night." Panic-stricken, she searched her mind for an excuse to leave. "I really am starved." She made a show of glancing at her wristwatch. "In fact, I think I forgot to eat lunch."

"Then let's take care of that right now." With the agility of a true sportsman, Shane got to his feet.

Carrie sighed her relief. Now all they had to do was get out of the beach house before stumbling upon Camille. Later she'd come up with some wild excuse to give her twin. No doubt, Camille would be furious and with just cause. But Carrie was confident she'd come up with some plausible explanation later.

Shane helped her into his BMW and walked around the front of the car. Carrie smiled at him shyly as he joined her and snapped the seat belt into place.

"You look good enough to kiss."

Quickly, Carrie looked out the side window. She wanted him to kiss her, desperately. But not now. And not here, with Camille within seconds of discovering them.

"Carrie." He touched the side of her face.

Feigning enthusiasm, she patted her abdomen. "My stomach is about to go on strike for lack of nourishment."

"Is that to say you'd rather eat than make love?" He frowned slightly.

"Feed me and we'll see how grateful I can be." She was flirting outrageously and loving it.

"Is that a promise?"

"We'll see."

Shane chuckled as he started the car and pulled onto the roadway. They weren't more than a hundred yards from the beach house when Camille's convertible came into view. Pretending to have found a piece of fuzz on her pant leg, Carrie took extreme care in re-

moving it, lowering her head. She prayed that Camille hadn't seen her.

By the time they reached the San Francisco waterfront, Carrie's mood had become buoyant. When
Shane parked the car, he paused and his eyes smiled
into hers. Even as he grinned, a slow frown formed.

"What's wrong?"

"Wrong?" He shook his head, clearing his
thoughts. "Nothing's wrong. I was just thinking that
I've never seen you glow like this. Your whole face has
lit up."

Her fluttering lashes concealed her reaction. "No
one has ever called me lovely before."

"I can't believe that."

"It's true."

He scooted in his seat, turning sideways. "You are,
you know. Gorgeous."

"Oh, Shane, I wish I knew how to react when men
pay me compliments." Her heart felt ready to burst
with love and appreciation. He'd given her a priceless
gift for which she'd always be grateful.

"You could kiss me," he suggested, only half-
serious.

"Here?" Lights shone all around them and the
sound of moving traffic drifted from the crowded
street.

Sensing her shyness, Shane lifted a lock of her hair
and let the silky smoothness slide through his fingers.
"There isn't anything I don't like about you," he admitted softly, his voice low and filled with wonder. "I
like the way your smile lights up your whole face." He
traced the corner of her eyes with his fingertips. His
mouth followed his hand, gently kissing each side of

her face. "Your eyes are so expressive. No one could
ever doubt when you're angry." With a tenderness she
wouldn't have associated with a man his size, Shane
leaned forward and brushed his lips over hers. He
paused, then kissed her a second time and then a third.
With each kiss, her mouth welcomed his, parting a
little more, moistening their lips as they twisted and
turned, gaining intensity.

He paused then, his mouth hovering a mere inch
above hers. "Feel good?"

For a heartbeat Carrie didn't move, didn't blink,
didn't even breathe. Answering him with words was
impossible, so she gently nodded her head. Each kiss
had wrapped her in a blanket of warmth and security.
She felt cherished and appreciated. Feminine and attractive. Seductress and seducer all in one.

"Oh, my sweet, Carrie." His breath felt hot against
her flushed cheeks. "All I wanted was to hold you, but
kissing you is like drinking ambrosia. I only yearn for
more." He moved his mouth to her throat where his
lips caressed the warm flesh there.

Carrie heard him draw in one deep breath as though
he needed to regain control of his emotions, then he
continued: "This isn't the best place to be thinking
what I am. Let's go have dinner."

Her hand against the back of his neck stopped him.
"I'm not hungry."

"Minutes ago you were famished."

"That was before." She tangled her fingers in his
thick hair. "I . . . like it when you kiss me."

"I like it too. That's the problem. And if we don't
stop now, it'll be a lot more than a few innocent
kisses."

The stark reality of their vulnerability to the world came as a truck passed, blaring its horn. The unexpected blast of sound brought Carrie up short. She blinked and broke free of Shane to press her hands over her face. Good grief, they were practically kissing in broad daylight with half the city looking on.

Noting her look of astonishment, Shane swallowed the growing need to laugh. Carrie never ceased to surprise him. She was a business woman who supported herself with her art and at the same time possessed a sophisticated innocence.

"Are you ready now?" He was looking in the direction of the seafood restaurant.

"I think so."

"Good." He hopped out of the car and came around for her. "By the way..." he hedged, instinctively knowing how dull his invitation would be. "There's an award banquet coming up at the end of next week. Would you be interested in attending it with me?" He tried to make light of it, but it was the high point of his career to receive the Frank Lloyd Wright Award. Wonderful for him, but deadly dull for anyone else.

"I read about the award you'll be receiving."

He looked almost boyish. "Then you'll go?"

"I'd consider it an honor."

"My great-aunt will be there as well. You won't mind meeting her, will you?"

How could she? Already she was falling in love with Shane. It would be only right to sit with his family when he was presented with this prestigious award. "I'll look forward to it."

"She's anxious to see you again."

His casual announcement shocked Carrie. They knew about her?

"From what I understand, you've already met my Aunt Ashley."

Instantly the picture of the astute older woman from Elizabeth Brandon's cocktail party flittered into Carrie's memory. "She's your aunt?"

"Does that shock you?"

"No. I'm just surprised." Realizing what she said, Carrie lightly shook her head. "I must have gone so long without food that my brain lacks the proper nutrients to think properly."

"Then I don't think we should dally any longer." Shane slipped his arm around her trim waist and led her toward Camille's favorite seafood restaurant.

"Where were you?" Camille demanded for the tenth time in as many minutes.

Carrie continued with the painting, doing her best to ignore her sister's anger. "Out to dinner. I'm sorry, Camille, really sorry."

"I thought you said he wanted to meet me."

"He does—someday."

"Then why..."

"It was a mistake. I've apologized, so can we please drop it."

Camille didn't look any too pleased. "I waited forty-five minutes for you." She crossed and uncrossed her arms, unable to disguise her indignation. "God only knows what could have happened to you. I had visions..." She left the rest unsaid.

Carrie felt terribly guilty. She set the brush aside and dropped her hand. "I realize it was a stupid thing to do."

"Where'd you go?" Camille insisted.

"Billy's."

"Billy's! You know how I love the food there." Her voice was low and accusing as though it should have been her and not Carrie. "I wouldn't see this mechanic...architect again," she warned.

"Why not?"

"He sounds fickle to me. You don't need that."

Carrie felt obliged to defend Shane. "He isn't, not really. He thought...he did want to meet you, but..."

"But?"

"But he decided that it was really me he was interested in."

"How nice," Camille grumbled.

"You have Bob."

"You can have him," she tossed back flippantly.

"Who? Bob or Shane?"

"Don't be silly. Bob's mine. I could care less about your friend who doesn't seem to be able to make up his mind. He sounds like bad news to me."

A secret smile touched the edges of Carrie's mouth. If Camille only knew, her song would be a whole lot different.

Chapter Six

Carrie went out with Shane three nights in a row. With each meeting she breathed in happiness and confidence and exhaled skepticism and uncertainty. Eventually, the time would come when he would have to meet Camille, but Carrie decided that there was no need to rush it. Nor did it matter that Shane believed she was the woman in the portrait.

Their first night out, Shane took her fishing in San Francisco Bay. Although neither got a single bite, it didn't seem to matter. The evening following the fishing expedition, they attended a concert in Golden Gate Park. Lying on a carpet of lush green grass with Carrie's head nestled in his lap, they listened to the sounds of Mozart. The next night they ate pizza on the beach and talked until well past midnight. Shane held and kissed her with a gentleness that never failed to stir her.

Between dates, Carrie painted Shane's portrait. She'd been right to believe this one painting would be a challenge beyond any other. She captured his likeness as she saw him: proud, intelligent, virile, vigorous, and overwhelmingly masculine. With every stroke of her brush she revealed her growing respect and love. Loving him had been inevitable. She'd known that from the first moment she'd peeked at him at the Dove Gallery the afternoon she'd delivered *No Competition*.

Camille complained about Carrie's absence early Thursday afternoon. "You're never home anymore. I hardly ever get to see you." Her twin's bottom lip pushed out into a clever pout. It amazed Carrie how nothing seemed to mar her sister's good looks. Not even a frown.

"You're seeing me now," Carrie announced as she delivered a small plate of Oreo cookies and two glasses of iced tea to the coffee table. She sat back and reached for a cookie.

"It's not the same."

"What do you mean?" Camille often came to Carrie with problems, but as far as Carrie could remember, she'd always been there for her sister. "Is something wrong between you and Bob?"

"What could be wrong? Everything's dandy."

Carrie realized that her sister was doing a poor job of acting. Camille's words were meant to disarm her, but they failed. Carrie had watched her relationship with Bob with interest. Her sister was falling in love. For the first time in her life, Camille was on unsteady footing, unsure of herself. Carrie could almost witness the small war going on inside her twin.

"I don't know about you," Carrie admitted on the tail end of a drawn-out yawn, "but I'm exhausted." The tiredness wasn't faked. Staying out with Shane until all hours of the morning was beginning to demand its toll.

A long pause followed and Carrie could feel her sister reassessing her. "I think Bob may want to cool things a bit," she admitted without looking at Carrie. "Naturally that choice is his. Either way is fine with me. There are plenty of other fish in the sea."

It sounded to Carrie as if Camille cared very much and struggled valiantly to disguise her emotions. "What makes you think that?"

Carrie appeared distracted, fiddling with the long spoon in the glass of iced tea. Carrie was well aware of how deeply troubled her sister was.

"Bob's done nothing really, but a woman senses these things."

"He must have said something." Idly Carrie reached for another cookie. Her bare foot was braced against the edge of the sofa.

"Not...really," Camille said without admitting anything.

"But you're convinced he wants to call off this relationship?" Carrie asked. She was well aware that Camille was leaving out all the necessary details. For a while, Carrie had thought Camille had found someone special. But this latest development didn't sound good.

Camille paused to take a sip of tea. Carrie noted that her twin didn't nibble on a single cookie. Oreos had long been their favorites. Having Camille ignore the treat was a sure sign of her distress. "He's still crazy about me, you know."

They all were. "I don't doubt it."

As though reading her sister's mind, Camille leaned forward and reached for an Oreo, holding it in front of her open mouth. "But maybe it's time I started going out with other men."

"Are you sure this is what you want?" She remembered how willing Camille had been to meet Shane. If she was truly in love with Bob, it wouldn't have mattered how many men showed an interest in her. Giving herself a hard mental shake, Carrie decided that she couldn't be overly concerned with her sister's love life when keeping track of her own demanded so much energy.

Camille bit into the Oreo. "By the way, when am I going to meet this new friend of yours?"

"Shane?" Carrie swallowed. Immediately she was reluctant to reveal anything about him.

"If that's his name."

"You'll meet him soon."

Camille stared straight through her. "That doesn't answer my question."

"I . . . don't know when you'll meet." Her words were raised and slightly defensive.

"You're not hiding him from me, are you?"

"Don't be silly." Carrie lowered her foot to the carpet and brushed off imaginary cookie crumbs from her lap. "You're not making any sense. I've always introduced you to my male friends." And lived to regret it, her mind tossed back.

"This one seems important."

Carrie shrugged. "Maybe. I'm like you when it comes to Bob. Shane's all right." So much for understatement! But she dare not let her sister know how involved her heart was. She couldn't trust Camille. Some days Carrie felt that her feelings for Shane must glow from every part of her. Even Elizabeth had commented how *healthy* Carrie looked lately. But, thankfully, Camille was so wrapped up in her topsy-turvy relationship with Bob that she failed to notice.

"Well, you certainly seem to be seeing a lot of him."

"I'm doing his portrait." That made everything sound so much more innocent.

"But you're together far more than necessary."

Carrie came to her feet and lifted her iced tea glass from the tray. "Why all the interest?"

"No reason."

"Then let's drop it, okay?"

Camille gave her an odd look. "Okay."

Her sister lingered around the beach house for another twenty minutes, asking questions occasionally. Camille had never been any good at disguising her curiosity. The time was soon approaching when Carrie would be forced to introduce her twin to Shane. Dreading the thought, Carrie quickly forced it to the back of her mind.

When Camille decided to leave, Carrie walked her out to her convertible. She felt wretched. Since their mother's death, she'd been the strong, bright twin. Lately, she'd been behaving like a fool. Love must do that to people, she decided. To her way of thinking, it was imperative to keep Camille away from Shane for as long as possible. Unreasonable? Probably. Selfish? All right, she admitted it. Scared? Darn right.

Camille pulled onto the highway, and as Carrie watched her sister leave, her discontent grew. Their conversation repeated itself in Carrie's troubled mind. She'd made her relationship with Shane sound as blasé as possible. Yet, in reality, she thought about him constantly. Not an hour passed that she didn't recall his quiet strength and his lazy, warm smile. She remembered the laughter they shared and how even small disagreements often became witty exchanges. They seemed to challenge each other's thoughts.

She loved his fathomless eyes which seemed to be able to look straight through her and know what she was thinking even before she voiced the thought.

Slowing, Carrie moved back into the house. Just thinking about Shane made her giddy with love. Somewhere, somehow, a long time ago, she had done something right to have deserved a man like Shane Reynolds. Now, if she could only hold on to him once he met Camille.

On the night of the award banquet honoring Shane, Carrie smoothed a thick curl of auburn hair away from her face. The eyeliner smeared and she groaned, reaching for a wash cloth, wiping it away to start once more. Again a thick curl of hair hung over her left eye. Irritably, she brushed it aside to guide the tip of the eyeliner across the bottom of her lid. A sense of panic filled her as she glanced at her gold watch for the tenth time in as many minutes. Oh Lord, this was the most important night of Shane's life and she was a half hour behind schedule.

Frantically waving her hand in front of her eye in an effort to dry the eyeliner, Carrie hobbled into her bedroom with one high heel on and the other lost somewhere under her bed . . . she hoped. Quickly she sorted through her closet for the lovely green dress she'd worn to Elizabeth's party. Shane had already seen her in it, but that couldn't be helped. The dress was the most flattering one she owned and she desperately wanted to make him proud tonight.

Of all the afternoons for Camille to show up unexpectedly, it would have to be this one all-important day. At three-thirty, her twin had descended on her doorstep, eyes red and puffy from tears. Sniffling, Camille had announced that she'd broken up with Bob and it was for the best and she really didn't care anyway. With that she'd promptly burst into huge sobs.

Carrie had no choice but to comfort her distraught sister. Camille needed her, and Carrie couldn't kick her out the door because she had an important date.

Carefully laying the silk dress across the top of the bed, Carrie prepared to slip it over her head. The dress was halfway down her torso when it stuck. No amount of maneuvering would get it to proceed further. Blindly walking around the room and hopping up and down didn't seem to help. It took her several costly moments to realize that the rollers in her hair were causing the hang-up.

"Damn, damn, damn," she muttered, pulling off the dress and in the process, turning it inside out. Trotting back into the bathroom, she ripped the hot rollers from her hair. By chance she happened to catch her reflection in the bathroom mirror and noticed that the eyeliner on the left eye had smeared. The right eye was bare; the job had only been half completed.

The sound of the doorbell shot through her like an electrical current, jolting her. "Please, don't let that be Shane," she pleaded heavenward, reaching for her old faded blue robe.

Naturally, it was Shane.

He stepped into the house looking so strikingly handsome in his tuxedo that just seeing him robbed her lungs of oxygen. She felt she'd burst with pride just looking at him. He was dashing. Stalwart. Devastating. She couldn't come up with another word to describe him. He was a man one expected to see with a beautiful woman. A Camille. Not a Carrie.

Dragging air into her constricting lungs, she froze. Springy curls hung around her head so that she resembled Eliza from *Uncle Tom's Cabin*.

Shane's stricken gaze collided with hers before lowering to the hastily donned terry cloth robe, left gaping open in the middle, revealing a peach colored teddy. His gaze rose to her stringy curls and quickly shot down to her feet. One foot was bare and the other propped in a two-inch high-heel sandal.

"Is it that time already?" she asked, her voice shaking as she strove for a light air.

"What happened?"

Carrie cinched the waist of the robe. "I'm running a tad bit late."

"I can see that."

Tears burned for release from the back of her eyes, but she refused to vent them. She'd wanted everything so perfect for Shane tonight.

"Listen, Shane, maybe it would be best if you went without me." She kept her hands at her side, hoping to appear lukewarm about the whole banquet. "As you can see I'm a long way from being ready."

He didn't so much as pause to consider her suggestion. "I want you there."

"Look at me," she cried, holding out her arms. She was a mess and all out of magic wands. For that matter her fairy godmother had recently retired. She was Cinderella long after midnight when the magic had worn off.

A crooked grin dented one side of his sensuous mouth. "I will admit that I'd prefer it if you wore a dress, but that's up to you."

"Don't joke," she cried. "This is too serious." Unable to hold back the stinging tears, she sniffled loudly. "Damn it, Shane, there's no way I can go now. Would you kindly be serious?"

"I've never been more so in my life." He pointed toward her bedroom. "Go do what's necessary and I'll phone Aunt Ashley and tell her we're running a few minutes behind schedule."

"Shane! It's going to take me six months to get everything in order."

"Take as long as you want." He claimed the sofa, sitting indolently and crossing his long legs. He propped both elbows against the back, looking as though he had all the time in the world. "I'm not in any hurry. As it is, these dinners are always stuffy affairs."

"But you're the guest of honor!"

"It's fashionable to be late."

"Oh, stop." She sank onto the sofa beside him. "I can't go."

Up until this point, Shane had found the whole proceeding humorous. But the tears shimmering in Carrie's soft eyes clearly revealed how grieved she was.

"Honey, look at me." His hand captured her chin and turned her face to him.

She resisted at first, not wanting him to see the tears that refused to be held at bay.

Lovingly, his finger traced the elegant curve of her jawline. "The reason this night is so important is because you can share it with me. I could care less what you wear."

"I refuse to embarrass you."

"You couldn't." The distress written in her eyes tore at his heart. Over the past few weeks he'd witnessed a myriad of emotions in her expressive eyes. She'd teased him, riled him. She'd given him an impudent sideways glance and stolen his heart several times over. He was so hopelessly in love with her that he didn't think his life would ever be the same without her now. He loved her wit and her intelligence and the way she could spar with him over one issue and then stubbornly defy him over another. Only this time he was determined to win. She was going to this awards banquet with him if he had to drag her every step of the way.

"Shane, don't make me, please."

Gently his hand smoothed away the tumbling curls from her troubled brow. "I want you with me."

"But . . ."

"Please." He said the word so tenderly that Carrie had no option.

Numbly she nodded, coming to a stand. She brushed the tears from her eyes. "I'll do the best I can."

"That's my girl."

Demanding that her frantic heart be still, Carrie worked with forced patience. Her eyeliner slid on smoothly and dried without smearing. With the hot rollers out of her hair, the dress glided over her head and whispered against her creamy skin. She wished she had more of a tan, wished her freckles would fade away, wished she was a ravishing beauty who would make him proud. A puzzled smile touched her lips as she reached for the brush to see what she could do with her hair. Shane should have a beautiful woman on his arm tonight. With everything that was in her, Carrie wanted to be that woman.

Thirty minutes later, she tentatively stepped into the living room. Shane was idly leafing through a woman's magazine.

"I think we can go now," she murmured, feeling a little like a fish out of water. For better or worse, she'd done her best.

Shane deposited the *Ladies' Home Journal* on the coffee table and glanced up. What he saw caused the breath to jam in his throat. Surprise exploded through his entire body. This wasn't the red-haired lovely who was more comfortable in faded jeans than a dress who stood before him, but a provocatively beautiful woman. He couldn't take his eyes from her. The transformation was little short of amazing. Her thick, luxuriant hair spilled over her shoulders. The silk clung to her slender hips and swayed gracefully as she walked toward him.

"Shane?"

"Good heavens, you're lovely." He'd forgotten. The night of Elizabeth Brandon's party he'd been struck at how beautiful she was. But that night he'd seen her from across the room. Now she stood directly in front of him and he felt as though he'd been hit with a hand grenade.

"Will I do?"

He could only nod.

"Well, don't you think we should be leaving? We're already thirty minutes late."

"Right." His hands fumbled in the silk-lined pocket of his trousers for the car keys. "I phoned Aunt Ashley. To save time, she insisted on taking a taxi and meeting us there."

"Remind me to thank her." Carrie shared a warm smile with him.

"I will." He offered her his elbow and turned to her. It took everything within him not to bend down and kiss her sweet mouth. What a surprise she was. A marvel. Just knowing her had enriched his life. Now all he needed to do was find some way to keep her at his side a lifetime.

"Mrs. Wallingford?" Carrie's apologetic eyes met the older woman's. "I hope you'll forgive me for this delay. It was inexcusable."

The low conversation hum of the party surrounded them. Shane had gone for drinks after seeing Carrie and his great-aunt seated at the round, linen-covered table closest to the award platform.

"Call me Ashley, my dear, and no apology is necessary. I've had days like that myself."

Carrie's gaze followed Shane as he progressed across the crowded floor. He didn't seem to be able to go more than a foot or two before he was stopped and congratulated.

Good-naturedly, Shane paused to talk with his colleagues, but his own gaze drifted back to Carrie and his aunt. He could hardly take his eyes from her, half afraid someone would walk away with her. She was breathtaking in that dress. A siren the gods had sent to tempt him. Well, it worked. He'd never wanted a woman more than he did Carrie. It astonished him that he'd only known her a month.

"You're in love with my nephew, aren't you?" Ashley Wallingford asked bluntly.

Carrie's gaze jerked away from Shane, aware that her heart must be boldly shining from her eyes. "Pardon?"

Ashley chuckled. "It's obvious."

Carrie twisted the gold link handle of her purse around her index finger. "I'd hoped it wasn't."

"I don't think Shane has guessed," the older woman reassured her. "He tells me you've been painting his portrait."

"Yes." Her eyes fell to the beaded purse resting in her lap. "He's an excellent subject."

"I can well imagine. The boy possesses a great deal of character. For a while there I didn't see much hope for him."

Carrie studied Shane's great-aunt, not sure she could believe what she was hearing. "Shane?"

"All he seemed to do was study. There wasn't any fun in his life." She chuckled softly. "He took everything so seriously. Responsibility weighed heavily on him. He's the only boy, you realize. After his father died, Shane did what he could to hold the family together. His mother was a frail little thing."

From conversations with him, Carrie knew that Shane's father had died the year Shane was a high school junior. His mother had followed a year or two later. His whole world had been ripped out from under him within the space of two years.

"He came to live with me then."

"He thinks the world of you." Carrie told her with pride.

Ashley Wallingford lightly shook her head. "It seems unfair that a boy should be faced with such unhappiness. His sisters are all married now." Abruptly changing the subject, Ashley continued. "There was a girl he loved, you know."

Carrie didn't. "He...hasn't mentioned anyone."

"She was a pretty thing. They met in college. To be honest, I thought they'd marry. But whatever happened, he didn't tell me. He didn't date for a long time afterward. For a while I assumed he gave up on women. Until now. It's time." The older woman's keen eyes assessed Carrie. "Her name was similar to your own. Connie, Candy...no, Camille. Her name was Camille."

Carrie thought her heart would pound right out of her chest. Dear Lord, could it have been her sister? Camille left a slew of battered hearts in her wake wherever she went. It was possible that Shane could be one. But...that didn't make sense. He wouldn't have purchased the portrait if it were Camille, would he?

"Carrie." Ashley Wallingford placed her hand over Carrie's. "You're looking pale. Was I wrong to have said anything?"

"No, of course not," she assured the kind woman hurriedly. "It would be highly unlikely that Shane would reach this age without ever having fallen in love. I can't be jealous of anyone who made him the man he is."

"You're very wise."

"Not really." Only intelligent enough to know that she couldn't look for problems in the past when the future held so many.

"Here we are," Shane said as he set down a round of drinks. "This place is a madhouse."

"I noticed," Carrie said with a small laugh.

"Everything should be starting any minute." He took the chair between his aunt and Carrie and reached for Carrie's hand. "I told you we'd arrive in plenty of time."

"The entire room sighed with relief the minute you walked in the door."

"You're exaggerating," he said.

"I'm very proud of you, Shane. Proud to know you and even more proud to be with you tonight." Emotion made Carrie's voice husky. "When I think back to all the things I said to you when we first met."

"You mean like, 'get lost'? You gave me a run for my money."

Carrie felt her heart swell with laughter. "My dear Mr. Reynolds, you're speaking as though the chase is over."

Shane tossed back his head and laughed heartily.

A tall, distinguished looking man approached the podium and the room grew quiet.

From its poor beginning, the evening took a turn for the better. The dinner was probably one of the best catered meals Carrie had ever eaten.

Following dinner, the award was presented and Shane rose to give his acceptance speech. Carrie barely heard a word of what he said. Instead her eyes scanned the huge audience that filled the ballroom. She saw for herself the admiration and respect on the faces of his peers. Even his aunt looked as proud as a peacock, her ample bosom seemingly puffed up as though to announce to the world that this man was her nephew. Poignant tears of happiness welled in the older woman's eyes. Carrie pretended not to notice as the delicate linen cloth was pressed to the corner of her sharp blue eyes.

As he spoke, a series of cameras flashed and television crews crowded into the already cramped room.

After the banquet, Shane was delayed by several people from the news media who stopped to ask him questions.

Shane kept his arm securely around Carrie's shoulder and within sight of his great-aunt. Ashley Wallingford found an old friend and the two discussed mutual acquaintances.

From the banquet room, Shane insisted they have a nightcap in the cocktail lounge off the hotel lobby. A small three piece band played music from the forties. The dance floor was crowded and it was apparent that this was a popular night club spot.

"Shall we?" Shane questioned his aunt and Carrie.

"You know I've always been an admirer of Glen Miller," Ashley murmured.

"Carrie?" He sought her response next.

"I'm game." The whole evening had been even more wonderful than she'd dared hope. As it was, she was far too keyed up to go home and sleep.

Shane found them a table and ordered their drinks when the cocktail waitress approached.

"Aunt Ashley, would you excuse us a moment?" Shane leaned over to ask his relative.

"Of course."

He scooted back his chair and reached for Carrie's hand. "I never could resist a good band."

Carrie's hesitation was only slight. She wasn't exactly light on her feet. Dancing had been another in a long list of items that Camille accomplished so much more proficiently than Carrie. "I hope you don't mind if I step on your toes."

"I don't."

"Brave soul," she said under her breath as she got to her feet.

"It wasn't my soul you warned me about," he returned, leading her onto the dance floor.

The music was a slow, sensuous ballad and Shane reached for her, holding her lightly against him. Carrie wound her arms around his neck, lifting her head to smile into his warm eyes.

"What was it you and my aunt were discussing so intently earlier?"

"She was letting me in on a few family secrets."

"Oh dear. And just which of my many indiscretions did she tell you about?"

"Does the name Camille mean anything to you?"

The laughter quickly faded from his eyes. "She was a long time ago. I was a kid."

"Should I be worried about her?"

"Hell, no. I think every man has to lose his heart once before he learns what it is to be a man."

"My only concern would be if she's still carrying it around with her."

"No." His laugh was dry. "She tossed it back at me."

Carrie's fingers smoothed the silver strands of hair along the side of his ear. Her heart filled with tenderness for the man who had given his love so completely only to lose it all. "Should I admit how pleased I am to know that?"

"I don't know, should you?" His hands pressed against the small of her back, bringing her intimately closer to him. His lips nuzzled her neck, pressing tiny kisses to the delicate slope of her throat.

Carrie melted against him, aware with every fiber of her being that she loved this man. His arms around her gave her the most secure feeling she'd ever known. Camille might flitter from one relationship to another, but Carrie was utterly content with one man—this man.

"Shane?" she muttered a minute later.

"Hmmm?"

"The music's stopped." The other couples on the dance floor were gradually returning to their tables.

"No, it hasn't," he countered. "I can still hear it loud and clear." He reached for her hand and pressed it over his heart. "Listen to what being near you does to me."

"Oh, Shane." She pressed her forehead to his shoulder, loving him all the more. "I hear wonderful music too."

"You do?" His eyes drifted open to stare into hers.

"I have from the moment you told me my freckles were beautiful."

"Everything about you is exceptional. Freckles," he paused to kiss her nose. "Eyes." His lips brushed over the corner of her eye. "But your sweet mouth takes the cake."

Artfully, Carrie managed to avoid his searching lips. She didn't know how to take him in this mood. He was serious and yet she could feel the laughter rumbling in his chest. She became painfully conscious that they were the only couple left on the floor. "Shane... people are looking at us."

"Let them look." His grip around her waist tightened.

"Your aunt..."

"Right," he murmured, dropping his arms. He led her back to the table.

Carrie was just about to sit when an all-too-familiar voice spoke from behind her. "Carrie, imagine seeing you here."

Dread settled like a lead balloon in the pit of Carrie's stomach. Slowly, she turned to face her twin.

Chapter Seven

Hello, Camille." Carrie felt as though her fragile world had suddenly been stricken by global disaster. The feeling was strangely melancholy. Pensive and sad. Her numb mind refused to function properly, to question what her sister was doing dancing when only hours before she'd been weeping uncontrollably. It took several painful seconds for Carrie to remember how quickly Camille rebounded from a broken heart. Bob was forgotten and once again Camille was on the prowl.

"So this is the man you've been keeping all to yourself." Smiling demurely, Camille moved forward, placing her hand on the rounded curve of her satin-clad hip as she studied Shane. She started with his handsome silver head, her eye roving downward with obvious interest. "Now I understand why."

Fleetingly, her gaze returned to Carrie. "Aren't you going to introduce us?"

"Yes...of course." She couldn't look at Shane, couldn't bear to see the admiration in his gaze as he recognized the face in the portrait. "Camille, this is Shane Reynolds and his great-aunt, Ashley Wallingford. Shane and Ashley, my twin sister."

"How do you do, Camille." Shane's voice revealed little of his thoughts. "Would you care to join us?"

So polite, so formal. Carrie didn't know him like this.

"I'd love it."

Sure she would, Carrie reasoned. Why not? Since early afternoon, Camille had been without a man and there was little doubt in Carrie's mind that Shane appeared overwhelmingly attractive. He was just what the doctor ordered for a slightly wounded heart. Carrie had thought he'd looked devastating only hours before. She'd watched with a heart full of pride as he accepted a prestigious award. Later, feeling blissfully content, she'd danced in his arms. Now Carrie was forced to stand by and watch her sister steal him away.

Like the gentleman he was, Shane pulled out Carrie's chair, but before she could reclaim her seat, Camille took it. The action was so typical of her twin's behavior that Carrie swallowed down an angry cry.

Without hesitating, Shane pulled an empty chair from another table and placed it next to his own. Carrie sat, her fists balled in her lap. She could feel Ashley's gaze studying her and did her utmost to appear poised.

"You must be the man who bought my portrait," Camille began, her voice raised and animated. "I was thrilled to hear that you liked it so much."

"Yes, I did buy it." Shane placed his arm along the back of Carrie's chair, but she received little comfort from the action. Camille had only started to pour on the charm. Once she gained momentum, few could resist her. Carrie didn't dare believe Shane would be the exception.

Leaning closer to him, Camille murmured, "I don't suppose Carrie's told you much about me."

"No, I can't say that she has."

Carrie refused to look in his direction.

"Carrie, dear," Ashley Wallingford whispered close to her ear. "Are you feeling all right?"

"I'm fine." Even her voice sounded strained and low. "Will you excuse me a moment?" she asked, coming to a stand. This could be the most important battle of her life and she wanted to check her war paint.

"Naturally." Camille answered for the entire group. "You run along and give me a chance to talk to these wonderful people."

The words were enough to give Carrie second thoughts, but she couldn't very well sit down and announce she wasn't going.

Refusing to run like a frightened rabbit, she crossed the room with her head held high, her steps measured and sure. She located the powder room without a problem and released a pent-up sigh the instant the door closed behind her. Her thoughts were in turmoil. She should have told Shane the truth about the portrait long before now. She admitted that much. But

if he cared half as much about her as she hoped, it
shouldn't matter. At least that was what Carrie told
herself while she repaired the damage to her makeup.
Her reflection showed wide, apprehensive eyes and a
flint-hard resolve. For the first time in her life she was
in love, and she'd move heaven and earth not to lose
Shane. Even if it meant fighting her own twin sister.

As Carrie approached the table, she noted that
Ashley Wallingford sat alone. Carrie's heart plum-
meted with defeat as her troubled gaze scanned the
dance floor. The self-confidence she'd worked so hard
to instill in the powder room vanished when she found
Camille's arms draped around Shane's neck. The
couple made only a pretense of dancing.

As much as possible, she tried to ignore them, re-
claiming her chair next to Shane's great-aunt.

"Do you feel better?" Ashley inquired.

"I did until a minute ago." Involuntarily, her gaze
darted back to the dance floor.

"I wouldn't have guessed you two were twins."

"Not many do," Carrie admitted. "Believe me, our
appearance isn't the only difference."

"I can see that."

The music ended and Camille returned to the small
table, her face flushed and happy. Apparently laughing at something humorous, she joined the other two
women and sobered.

"I like your friend, Carrie," she admitted boldly,
smiling up at Shane. "You should have introduced us
weeks ago. Isn't that right, Shane?"

His response barely penetrated through the wave of
pain that assaulted Carrie. Shane was already Camille's, and in record time. Her twin had once bragged

that most men succumbed in less than a week. Carrie had never seen Camille work so fast. She was out to capture Shane in one evening.

"I have always adored men with silver hair," Camille continued, sharing a secret smile with Shane.

"It's a family trait," Ashley Wallingford stated blandly. "All the Reynolds men gray prematurely."

"How interesting." But Camille barely glanced in the older woman's direction. "I still can't get over sweet Carrie dating such a handsome man."

"Thank you," Shane returned politely. "And I'd say that beauty runs in the family."

Camille's incredulous gaze flew to Carrie in disbelief. "Yes, yes it does, although most everyone believes I received more than my fair share in that department. But Carrie's so talented that no one seems to notice her...minor deficiencies."

Shane was angry. Angry with this clinging twin of Carrie's who possessed all the sensitivity of corn husks and angry with Carrie. He loved her and had for weeks. It was a shock to learn she hadn't been completely honest with him, and a disappointment as well. He wouldn't have believed she was capable of such deception. He wanted to shake her and in the same breath reassure her. He did neither.

"But then you've seen lots of me already," Camille continued undaunted. "After all, you did buy my portrait."

"He thought it was me." Carrie realized the instant she opened her mouth that she should never have spoken.

"You've got to be kidding." Camille's features were frozen with disbelief. "Why that's absurd. We look nothing alike."

"We *are* twins."

"But not identical twins," Camille countered.

"There are similarities," Shane inserted. "But now that I see the two of you together, I realize how wrong I was to have made the comparison. Carrie's nothing like the portrait."

Carrie paled and a rock settled where her heart had once been. Without much effort, Camille had managed to wrap Shane around her little finger. She would have thought better of him. But this was only round one and Carrie hadn't even put on her gloves yet. She loved this man and she wasn't giving him up quite this easily. She'd allowed her sister to snatch other men from her grasp and Camille hadn't even been trying. This time she was. In the past, no one had mattered as much as Shane.

"It's been a long tiring evening. It's time we got you home, Aunt Ashley," Shane exclaimed, pushing back his chair.

"I do feel a bit drained," the older woman responded. "But it's been most enjoyable. All of it."

Carrie stood up. Her evening bag was clenched so tightly in her hand that her fingers grew numb. "Yes, it has been great," Carrie concurred. "Most of the time," she whispered under her breath.

If Camille could dish it out, she should learn to take it as well. Although from the looks that Shane was giving her, Carrie would've done well to have kept her mouth shut. Too late she remembered the protective reaction Camille often evoked in men.

"I know you'll want to get in touch with me," Camille said and smiled boldly up at Shane. "I'm sure Carrie will be happy to give you my number. But then, you don't need to ask. I'm in the book."

"It was nice to have met you."

"A pleasure."

Wordlessly the small party of three left the hotel. The valet brought Shane's vehicle around and soon they were driving through the well-lit city streets. The silence inside the car was thicker than any fog San Francisco had ever seen. Shane drove to his aunt's home in Nob Hill first. Even before they arrived, Shane refused an invitation for them to come inside for another nightcap. Carrie couldn't have agreed more. She enjoyed his Aunt Ashley and knew that this perceptive lady was well aware of Camille's game. Carrie only hoped that Shane was just as intuitive.

Once in Nob Hill, Shane saw his aunt safely to her door and returned a couple of minutes later.

"Well?" he said once he'd climbed back inside the car.

"Well what?"

"Aren't you going to explain?"

"About the portrait? No." Carrie couldn't see confusing the issue at this late date. Everything should be fairly obvious. "However, if you're seeking an apology, you have it. I should have been honest about the painting. In light of what's happened this evening, my regrets have doubled."

Shane thought about her answer a moment before asking, "You feel insecure next to your sister, don't you?"

"Insecure?" Carrie tried to laugh off the truth. "Heavens, why should I?"

"You tell me."

Shane wouldn't be fooled easily and Carrie quickly abandoned her guise. "All right. I'm insecure. I have good reason. Camille's stolen away more boyfriends than I care to count. Most of them without even trying. I'd hoped..." She hesitated, unsure of the wisdom of revealing her feelings.

"You hoped what?"

"Simply that you'd show a lot more character than the others. Apparently I was wrong."

"Just what do you mean by that?"

"You're behaving like a besotted fool. Enthralled with her beauty. Drinking in her every word. Don't you think I already know that I'm a poor second next to Camille?" She was lashing out now, angry. "You told me I was lovely and I was fool enough to believe you."

"You are."

"But Camille's perfect, and I noticed you certainly didn't waste any time sampling her abundant charms. I would have thought that—"

She wasn't allowed to finish. "Just what the hell do you mean by that?" Every second of this conversation was irritating him more. He wasn't particularly fond of Carrie's twin sister and he didn't like the sound of these accusations either.

"I saw the way the two of you were dancing. Good heavens, you looked like you were glued together. It was disgusting."

"Was it so disgusting when I was dancing with you?"

"No," she answered honestly. "But then you've known me longer than thirty seconds." The last thing she wanted was to argue with Shane, but her outrage grew and grew until venting it made good sense. "Maybe...maybe you've always yearned for a Camille. Wasn't that the name of your first love? Well, now you've found her. Perhaps not her, but another who should fit the bill nicely."

"Would you kindly shut up!"

"No. Perhaps you think I'm jealous. All right, I'll admit it. I am. But I thought so much more of you than this. If it's Camille you want, then fine. You're welcome to her. It's lucky you met her when you did. She's between men at the moment, and you'll suffice nicely. But when you've had your fun, don't come back to me. I never have appreciated Camille's rejects."

Shane's eyes narrowed to points of steel. He looked as though he didn't trust himself to speak. Instead, he started the car and pulled onto the street. His hand compressed around the steering wheel so hard that it threatened to collapse under the grinding pressure.

They didn't exchange another word during the thirty minute drive to the beach house. With every mile, Carrie's contrition mounted. She regretted each impulsive word. Only a few minutes before, she'd been determined to fight for Shane, and now she was practically throwing him into Camille's arms.

He didn't shut off the engine when he reached her beach house. His hands remained on the steering wheel and he stared straight ahead.

Carrie's fingers grasped the door handle, prepared to depart. Shane was angry, angrier than she'd ever known him to be. She'd been hurt by his thoughtless actions and in her pain, she'd lashed out at him. She drew in a tortured breath.

"Good night, Shane," she murmured in a small, distracted voice. "I'm very sorry that I ruined your special night. But I want you to know how proud I am of your accomplishments, and so very pleased you brought me to the award ceremony with you. I'll...I'll always remember that." Sick with defeat, the taste of failure and disillusionment coating her mouth, Carrie slipped from the car and hurried into the cottage.

For ten minutes Shane didn't move. His instincts told him to drive away and not look back. He was tired and emotionally drained. But the sound of Carrie's tormented voice echoed around the interior of the car to haunt him. He couldn't leave her like this. He loved her. But damn it, she'd lied to him, deceived him. He needed time to sort out his reaction to that.

Angrily, he shifted the car into reverse and roared back onto the highway. They both needed space to bandage their injured pride.

Sitting inside the house, Carrie's head reared back when she heard Shane's car leave the driveway. For a few minutes she'd thought he might not go. But that hope died when he revved his car engine and pulled away. She knew they both regretted the harsh words. If only he hadn't been so willing to dance with Camille. And what they were doing could hardly be termed dancing. Her anger mounted with the memory. Unable to contain it, she paced the narrow living room more furious now than before.

If Shane wanted Camille, then Carrie would let him go without a backward glance. Wash her hands of him

without remorse. Cast him aside and be grateful she'd
learned what she had before she was completely in love
with him.

It's too late, her heart taunted. *Far too late.*

Sleeping was impossible. Her mind spun out of
control with questions demanding answers that she
didn't have. The bedroom walls seemed to press in
around her. An hour after retiring, Carrie abandoned
the effort of even pretending she could sleep.

As she often did when her thoughts were too heavy
to escape with slumber, Carrie walked down to her
private beach with a steaming mug of spiced tea.

Moonlight splashed against the sandy shore. Its
golden rays illuminated the night. There was a solace
here that she could find nowhere else. For a long time,
Carrie had thought the one great love of her life would
be this beach. Now she knew how wrong she'd been.
The only love of her life was Shane Reynolds and if
she wasn't careful, she was going to lose him. It might
be too late already.

Sitting on the thick bed of sand, she pulled her legs
up against her chest and wrapped her arms around her
knees. The night was cloudless, the stars brilliant, like
rare glittering jewels on a background of dark velvet.

"I thought I'd find you here."

Startled, she gasped at the sound of the unexpected
intruder. The moonlight revealed Shane standing beside her. He'd discarded his tie. The top three buttons
of his starched tuxedo shirt were unfastened, revealing curling silver chest hair.

"Do you mind if I join you?"

"Please do." Carrie's heart was singing and she had
trouble finding her voice.

Shane lowered his bulk to the sand next to her. "You couldn't sleep?" He made the statement a question.

"No. You neither?"

"I didn't try. I parked a couple of miles down the road and stopped to think."

At least they were speaking to each other. However, their conversation was more like that of polite strangers.

"I tried," Carrie admitted.

"I would have thought you'd paint."

"No." Slowly she shook her head. "Contrary to popular myth, art demands too much concentration. And according to Camille, I make as much money as if I worked a nine-to-five job!" Carrie instantly regretted mentioning her twin's name. Shane's expression tightened and she glimpsed a bit of his frustrated anger. Gathering her resolve, Carrie gripped her arms more securely around her bent legs. "I honestly am sorry for not telling you about Camille."

"I wish you had, but having met your sister explains a great deal." His eyes captured hers, demanding that she return his gaze. "I suppose her portrait in my office is why you bolted that day."

Carrie's wry grin was lopsided. She nodded, all the more ashamed now. "Camille's always been the beauty in the family. You were right when you said—"

"I can't believe you." Hands buried deep within his pockets, Shane paced the area in front of her, kicking up sand. "If you'd only told me."

"I know."

"All this time, I thought . . ."

"I said I was sorry." Carrie felt worse. Shane had every reason to be angry. But he didn't understand what having a twin sister like Camille had meant in her life. However, now when he was upset with her deception wasn't the time to enlighten him. Given time, he'd see it all.

"I didn't mean the things I said earlier." She tried again, wanting to set things right between them.

"I know that, too."

"I was . . . jealous when I saw you dancing with Camille." Carrie doubted he knew what it had cost her to admit that.

"She was the one who invited me to dance. A gentleman doesn't refuse a lady."

Somehow Carrie already knew that as well, but had hoped Shane would have found a way to extract himself. He hadn't, and that seemed to prove that he wasn't as immune to Camille as he'd like her to believe.

With her head drooping, Carrie waited as the seconds ticked by. She yearned for Shane to take her in his arms and erase the hurts and anxieties of the evening. Finally she raised her eyes to him. "Shane," she whispered achingly, "would you please hold me?"

He reached for her, slipping an arm around her shoulders and catching the side of her chin with his index finger, lifting her mouth to receive his kiss.

Carrie twined her arms around his neck and pressed against him. She yearned to wipe the thought of Camille from his mind and replace it instead with the warmth of her love. With a smothered moan, she met his mouth in a hungry kiss, glorying in the feel of his lips over hers.

Her body molded to the hard contours of his chest. His hand pressed possessively on her back, sliding up and down her spine as he gathered her pliable form closer to his.

"Let's never argue again," she pleaded, breathlessly.

"Are you kidding? When we can make up like this?"

Without exactly knowing how it happened, Carrie discovered that she was sitting on his lap, her arms draped around his neck. "I was hoping that we could do this frequently without needing the incentive of cross words."

"Agreed." His mouth brushed hers. "Do you have any idea how good you taste?"

"You too." Her mouth slanted over his, loving the way his warm lips moved to part hers. His tongue played with hers, darting in and out in an erotic game of tag. Slowly the kiss altered, becoming excruciatingly slow and deliberate.

Shane twisted so that Carrie was pressed against the beach and he lay half on top of her. A thick bed of sand cushioned the change in their positions. Briefly, he brought up his head, waiting for her to tell him to stop.

Carrie couldn't. She loved him so much and she was so afraid of what the future held for them. She couldn't bear it if Camille were to whisk him away. Not when she'd been waiting a lifetime for him.

With limitless patience, Shane dipped his mouth to hers again and again. Her lips parted in eager delight, welcoming the gentle thrust of his tongue. He skimmed the inner lining of her mouth, their tongues meeting tentatively at first, then mating lingeringly.

Carrie was breathless with wonder and pleasure. He tasted delicious. Like mint and man and everything that could ever be good. She clenched a handful of his hair, fusing his mouth all the tighter to her own. Still caught in the rapture, Carrie was astonished to discover that Shane had unfastened the buttons of her blouse. Reverently, his hands sought the fullness of her breasts and her eyes fluttered closed at the exquisite pleasure he gave her.

"Oh, Carrie," he groaned and seemed unable to say more. "You're beautiful. So very beautiful."

Unbidden tears moistened the corner of her eyes. "I'm not." She was shocked to hear the sound of her own voice.

Shane raised his head and studied her, then carefully, with the most tender care, he covered each breast, cupping each one. His eyes drifted back to her and held her gaze for what seemed forever. "Oh yes, you are, my love." Then gently, so very gently, he brushed his thumb over the sensitive nipples.

Carrie whimpered and closed her eyes to the consummate pleasure of his touch.

Again his mouth found hers, tasting, kissing, licking until Carrie thought she would go mad with longing. She was deliciously warm and suddenly she was cold. Her eyes shot open at the unexpected shaft of cool breeze. Shane was off her and lay with his eyes squeezed shut, taking in deep, even breaths.

"Shane," she cried, her voice tight with worry. "What's wrong? Did I hurt you?"

He jerked his head in rapid response. "No, love. I'm just clearing my head."

"But—"

"Shhh." He sat up and rubbed a hand across his face. The hardest thing he'd ever done was break away from Carrie at this moment. Dear Lord, he wanted her. But now wasn't the time. Not when she was weak with insecurities. When they made love, he didn't want any shadows lingering between them. Only time would prove he had no interest in her twin sister.

"It would be too easy to love you completely," he breathed out brokenly, fighting for composure. He claimed her hand and kissed the inside palm. "But neither of us is ready for that just yet. When the time is right, we'll know it and there won't be any doubts."

Doubts! She didn't have any doubts. She loved him, wanted to spend the rest of her life with him. For a time, she'd believed that was what Shane was thinking too. But he'd met Camille and now unanswered questions abounded. The only thing left to do was confront Camille. And Carrie was determined to do that at the earliest moment.

"Carrie." Camille slid into the opposite side of the booth where Carrie was waiting. "This is a surprise. It isn't every day that my sister calls and invites me to lunch."

Carrie's smile was forced. "We should do it more often."

"Especially if you're buying," Camille joked. She picked up the menu and scanned the contents, quickly making her choice. "I had a grand time with Shane the other night."

"Oh?"

"He's so good-looking. Where'd you meet him?"

"He bought a painting."

"Of course," Camille giggled. "Mine."

With limitless patience, Carrie set the menu aside. Her stomach was in turmoil, but she'd order and make the pretense of eating. The time was long overdue for a heart-to-heart talk with her only sibling.

The waitress came and took their order. Not surprisingly, they both asked for the same thing. Spinach salad with the dressing on the side. They were alike just as much as they were different, although they always seemed surprised when they discovered it.

The waitress left after filling their coffee cups.

"I always enjoy a good spinach salad," Carrie felt obligated to defend her choice.

"Me, too."

"It . . . seems that there's another thing we share."

"What's that?" Camille spread the linen napkin across her lap and glanced up expectantly.

"I'm going to be honest with you, Camille. I love Shane Reynolds."

Camille blinked, but revealed none of her feelings. "Congratulations. Is he in love with you?"

"I think so."

"How nice."

"Camille, I didn't ask you to lunch to discuss the weather. I want to talk about Shane."

Her twin's look was only slightly smug. "I suppose you want to ask my advice."

"Yes." Carrie felt like shouting. "But first I want to give you some. For the first time in my life I'm honestly in love. Please have the common courtesy to

keep your hands off." So much for tact and subtlety.
Any attempt at diplomacy was wiped out. All morning Carrie had rehearsed what she wanted to say. Yet
the minute Camille had ordered the spinach salad,
Carrie knew she was in trouble. They both liked the
same things, and now apparently they also liked the
same man. Already Carrie could see the long lonely
years stretched out before her. The one romance of her
life foiled by a spinach salad.

To make matters worse, Carrie discovered that she
was shaking from the inside out. She dared not reach
for her coffee. The hot liquid would slosh over the
edges of the cup.

"I can't help it if he's attracted to me," Camille
countered.

"You practically threw yourself at him."

"Oh, honestly, Carrie, I wouldn't do that. He was
your date."

"Do you notice the way you put that in past tense?
The minute you appeared, anyone would have been
hard pressed to say whose date he was. You were all
over him on the dance floor."

Camille looked dumbfounded. "You're overreact-
ing."

"No." Her hand closed around the fork as she
dropped her gaze to the table top. "All right, maybe I
am. But for the first time in my life, I'm head over
heels in love and I don't want to lose him."

"Carrie." Camille looked shocked. "Do you think
I'm going to try to steal Shane away from you?"

"I don't know."

"I wouldn't. Honest. He's cute and everything, but if he's that important to you, then I'll forget him. He's history."

Carrie was so relieved that she felt like crying. "I'm sorry about you and Bob."

"Don't be. He was getting too serious." Quickly Camille changed the subject, lowering her eyes. "So you're in love. That's great."

"I think so. Shane hasn't said anything—yet. But I think he will. I mean . . . well, I feel that he loves me too."

Camille laughed lightly. "It's such a surprise, you know."

"What is?"

"You falling in love first. I always thought it would be me." She raised the coffee cup and poised it in front of her mouth. "But this does create one problem."

"What's that?"

"Shane phoned me earlier and invited me to his house this evening. I suppose you'd prefer it if I didn't go now, wouldn't you?"

Chapter Eight

"Shane phoned you?" Carrie repeated numbly, trying to assimilate the news and its meaning.

"First thing this morning." Camille nodded for emphasis. "I was really surprised. Do you mind if I go?"

"He didn't say what it was about?"

"No."

Their salads arrived and Camille smiled her appreciation to the young waitress who delivered their order. Reaching for the dressing, Camille ladled it over the top of the crisp spinach leaves topped with fried bacon and slivers of hard boiled egg.

Carrie couldn't have taken a bite if her life depended on it. Her thoughts were in chaos. There could be no logical explanation for Shane to contact her sister. Especially knowing the way Carrie would react. If he'd been looking for a way to hurt her, then he'd gone straight for the jugular. He knew her feelings. That night on the beach, she'd bared her soul to Shane. She'd told him of her insecurities. He knew how she felt about Camille's beauty. Now his response was to contact her twin. She'd been fooled. Shane Reynolds wasn't the man she'd thought him to be.

"Well, what should I do?" Camille asked between bites. "I don't want to upset you, but on the other hand, I don't want to be rude to Shane either."

"Go." At Camille's dubious glance, Carrie added, "I mean it. There are no commitments between Shane and me. If he wants to see you, then fine. Great. Terrific. Make the most of it. I would."

"Carrie." Camille said her sister's name softly. "I've seen you use that tone of voice before, and it usually means trouble."

"What tone of voice?" Pride demanded that she reach for her fork and plow into her spinach salad with the gusto of a starving woman. On the inside she was dying, but a smile lit up her face and no one would ever know. Certainly not her sister and definitely not Shane.

Camille chatted easily over their lunch, discussing her job and a new dress she picked up on sale. She commented that she'd probably wear the pale blue summer dress when she went to Shane's that evening. She paused, her cheeks turning a light shade of pink when she realized she was distressing her sister. Quickly, she changed the subject.

The rest of their lunch passed in silence. Camille spoke after the waitress brought the bill to the table. "Maybe it isn't such a good idea for me to visit Shane, after all."

"I think you should. Otherwise, you'll always wonder," Carrie told her. It was the most she'd said since Camille had dropped her little bomb. Somehow Carrie managed to swallow down her lunch, but the effort had been Herculean, and her stomach would ache afterward.

Carrie and Camille parted outside the restaurant on the sidewalk, each going their separate ways. On the drive back to the beach house, Carrie noted the thick clouds swollen with rain.

Once home, she moved directly into her studio and sat in front of the canvas that revealed Shane's serious eyes and prominent facial features. She was proud of this portrait. She'd outdone herself. Her love shone with every stroke of the brush as she'd painted the face of the man she cared for so much. Loved, yes. Trusted—she didn't know.

Picking up the easel, she checked her answering machine for messages and punched the tape back in before starting to work. The phone rang three times, but Carrie didn't stop, preferring to paint uninterrupted. She was close to being done with this portrait and she felt it was imperative to finish it soon. Although it was her best work to date, she wished she'd never agreed to paint Shane. Having those lovingly familiar eyes follow her every time she moved was almost more than she could bear.

She worked straight through dinner and well into the evening. The portrait was done. She'd finished, and was exhausted...mentally and physically. While she cleaned her brushes, she played back her telephone messages: "Carrie, it's Shane. I'm just calling to see if you're free for dinner tomorrow? If I don't hear back from you, I'll assume that we're on for seven.''

Carrie snorted. She wasn't about to call him. He could show up at seven, but she wouldn't be here. She could say one thing for Shane, he sure made the rounds—Camille tonight and her the next. Between the two of them, his social calendar could be filled for the next six months.

The tape continued with the second message: ''Carrie, it's me. I've thought about it all afternoon. I'm not going to meet Shane. You love the guy. He's yours. I don't want to do anything to disrupt your plans with him. You're my sister and I am not going to take him away.''

The third message was Camille again. ''Listen, don't be mad. Oh, this is Camille, you know I hate these stupid machines. I wish you'd answer the phone like everyone else. Anyway, I've changed my mind. I am going to meet Shane. I thought it over and well...there could be a very innocent motive behind this get-together.''

''Sure!'' Carrie murmured under her breath.

''Anyway'', Camille continued, ''I'll call you first thing in the morning and let you know how everything went.''

Yawning on her way into the bedroom, Carrie peeled the T-shirt over her head and reached for her Captain America pajamas. Heavens, she was tired. A glance at the clock radio on her night stand told her it was three a.m. Carrie stared at it in disbelief. She'd worked that long? Amazing. But the portrait was done and that was what mattered. Her commitment to Shane was complete.

The phone rang sometime early, disturbing her sleep, but Carrie couldn't be dragged from her peaceful slumber and didn't bother to answer it.

She woke around ten. Bright sunshine crept into the bedroom, its golden light making further sleep impossible. Grumbling, she stumbled out of bed, yawning as she lazily walked into the kitchen.

Her dreams had been so delicious that she hated to wake and face the chill of reality. Her heart was heavy as she flipped the switch on the telephone recorder.

"It's me. Sorry I'm calling so early, but I'm on my way to work and I wanted to tell you how everything went last night with Shane. You're right, Carrie, he really is a wonderful man. I think . . ."

Viciously, Carrie cut off the tape. She didn't want to hear it. Not any of it.

Having gotten off to a late start, the day was half gone by the time Carrie showered and dressed. Lackadaisically, she scrambled a couple of eggs. She was about to pour those into the pan when a loud knock sounded against her front door.

For a moment she toyed with the idea of ignoring it and hoping whoever was there would simply go away. She wasn't in the mood to buy anything, nor did she feel up to entertaining company.

Another knock followed, and groaning, Carrie walked across the carpet intent on sending away whoever was there as quickly as possible.

"Yes," she said in her most stiff, unfriendly voice. The man standing in front of her was only vaguely familiar. She'd met him once, but she couldn't remember when or where. He looked terrible. His clothes were wrinkled as though he'd slept in them. He was also badly in need of a shave.

"I'm sorry to bother you. Hell, I probably shouldn't have come." He buried his hands in his pockets and glanced at the sky. "You don't even remember who I am, do you?"

"No," she admitted honestly.

"Bob Langston. We met briefly a couple of months ago."

"Oh, sure," Carrie said and relaxed. "You're Camille's Bob."

He blanched. "Not anymore, I'm afraid."

"Would you like to come in for a cup of coffee?"

"If you're sure it's no problem."

"I wouldn't have asked you in otherwise." She unlatched the screen and held it open for him. "In fact I was just about to fix some breakfast. Bob looked as if he could use a decent meal as well.

"Please don't let me stop you."

"If you don't mind, we can talk as I cook."

"Sure."

He followed her into the kitchen and took a chair. Carrie poured a cup of coffee and brought it to him. "Cream? Sugar?"

"No, this is fine. Thanks."

He looked so dejected and unhappy that Carrie felt sorry for him. She had met him months ago, but his appearance was drastically altered from that first meeting. Well, she probably didn't resemble any beauty queen this morning herself. If he was looking for someone to commiserate with, she was readily available.

Without asking, she added a couple of extra eggs to the bowl and whipped them with a fork until the mixture was frothy. "I suppose you want to talk about Camille."

His shoulders sagged forward as his large hands cupped the coffee cup. "She broke it off. I still can't believe it."

"Did Camille give you any reason?" She'd been so teary that day, Carrie hadn't gotten the story straight.

"Tons, but none of them made sense."

A small smile edged up one side of Carrie's mouth. "I know what you mean."

"To make matters worse, she's already seeing another man. Some rich guy on Nob Hill. She went to his house last night."

"You...followed her?" If he was about to reveal the details of Camille's meeting with Shane, then Carrie didn't want to hear about it.

Bob was decent enough to look ashamed of his actions. "Yes. That has to rank right up there as unforgivably stupid."

Carrie couldn't recall much of Camille's rationalizations when she announced that she and Bob had split. From what she did remember, Carrie thought Camille had said Bob was the one who decided to call things off.

"Maybe you'd better start at the beginning." She added a slice of butter to the hot pan and when it had melted, she poured in the eggs.

"There's not really much to tell. We'd been seeing quite a bit of each other. I was beginning to think that maybe we should think about getting married. We even talked about it a couple of times. Then out of the blue, Camille says that she feels we need to see less of each other. I was furious. Good grief, I was carrying around a diamond ring in my pocket, looking for a romantic minute to slip it on her finger, and she says something crazy like that. I came unglued.''

"That's funny because it seems to me that she said you called it off."

"Me?" Bob's face was a study of incredulousness. "That's insane. I love Camille. I have for months, but she'd taken me on this wild-goose chase almost from day one."

"And last night when you followed her, Camille was going to Shane Reynolds's house. Shane and I have been seeing a lot of each other."

"So it was all innocent." His relief was evident.

As best she could, Carrie swallowed down her pain. "I . . . I don't know."

"What do you mean?"

With her back to him, Carrie stirred the cooking eggs. "I did a portrait of Camille a while back and Shane bought it."

"Hell, I wish I'd known about it. I would have loved to have it." He said this absently, his voice thick with regret. "I want to marry her, you know. I've waited a long time to settle down. I just never believed that the woman I love would walk away from me like this." He shook his head as though to clear his thoughts. "Sorry. Go on."

"There's not much to tell. Shane bought the painting. He says he did it because . . . well, he thought it was me." She felt a little crazy to even suggest something like that now, when the differences between the two sisters were so prominent.

"I can understand that," Bob murmured. "You are sisters. The coloring's a bit different, but you two resemble each other quite a bit. In subtle ways."

"Really?" Even though Shane had told her the same thing, Carrie had trouble believing it.

"Sure."

"Anyway, I . . . I never corrected Shane's impression. Then we happened to bump into Camille, and he learned the truth."

"So you assume that Shane is more interested in Camille?"

"What else can I think? He contacted her."

"And she went? Knowing how you feel about Shane?" His brown eyes hardened.

Carrie nodded. "I told her I didn't mind."

"That sister of yours needs to be taught a lesson."

"As far as I'm concerned it's Shane who should learn a thing or two." The room filled with an electric silence. Carrie dished up the scrambled eggs and brought them to the table. But neither of them ate.

"Well, what are we going to do about it?" Bob asked.

"I don't know."

"Shane and Camille have no business being together."

"It could all be innocent," Carrie felt obliged to say, although she could offer no plausible reason Shane would contact Camille. "Like us being together now." The instant the words left her mouth, an idea shot into Carrie's troubled mind. "You know, I may have something here."

"What?" Bob leaned forward expectantly.

"We know our meeting is strictly innocent, but Shane and Camille don't."

"What's that got to do with anything?"

"They could see us together and wonder. In fact, it would probably do them both good."

"I couldn't agree with you more." Bob's eyes shone with a delighted twinkle. "I think I could come to like you as a sister-in-law," he said, reaching for his fork.

Breakfast took on more appeal for Carrie as well. "Here's what I think we should do."

When Bob returned several hours later, he'd shaved and his hair was neatly trimmed and combed back, revealing strong male features. Carrie could understand why her sister had found him so attractive.

"You're sure Camille will be at Billy's?" Carrie asked.

"Positive." He chuckled under his breath. "You know I'm almost looking forward to this."

"Me, too."

"Where to first?"

"Shane's. I want to deliver this portrait."

Bob's gaze clashed with hers. "I know the way."

Bob waited while Carrie locked her front door. Then he carefully secured Shane's portrait in the trunk of his car, and helped Carrie into the front seat.

During the drive into the city, they talked and joked like old friends. Carrie found it easy to talk with Bob, and was furious with her sister for having led such a good man down a rocky road.

As Bob claimed, he was well acquainted with the route to Shane's home on Nob Hill.

When he pulled into Shane's driveway, he turned to her. "Do you want me to go with you?"

"No, I'd prefer to do this on my own."

"Okay, but if you need me, just say the word."

"Don't worry, I will."

Once again, he helped her with the large canvas. Once she was at the door, Bob returned to the car, leaning against the bumper.

Smiling, Carrie rang the bell and waited.

Shane appeared almost immediately. "Carrie, this is a surprise."

Her answer was a wry grin. "I only have a minute. I wanted to drop off the portrait."

"I would have picked it up myself if I'd known you were finished."

Carrie noted the way his gaze darted past her to Bob. He picked up the canvas and studied it, his approval showing in his eyes. "This is marvelous."

"Thank you."

"Come in," he offered, "I didn't mean to keep you standing out here."

"I can't, thanks. I've got a dinner date."

"I thought we were going out tonight." Again his eyes shot past her to Bob, waiting in the driveway. "I assumed—"

"I'm sorry, Shane, but I'd already made plans."

By the way his mouth compressed into an angry line, Carrie could tell that he was striving to keep his temper. His eyes raked over her, then past her to Bob.

"I felt we had an understanding, Carrie."

"To be honest, so did I," she said, revealing for the first time some of her own pain. "I . . . I've never felt closer to anyone than to you that night on the beach."

"What happened to change that?"

"That's more a question for you than me." To her horror her voice cracked. "Really," she said and took a step backward. "I've got to be going."

"Carrie." Shane set the portrait aside and followed her onto the porch. "I don't understand."

"I don't know how you can say that. You're the one who's confused things. It's you who can't seem to make up your mind which twin sister interests you."

Shane was certain Carrie was referring to his meeting with Camille, and was slightly annoyed. If she'd stop playing the rejected lover, this would soon be resolved. "Carrie, I can explain if you'd like to listen."

Backing away from him, she winced at the blaze of love and tenderness that shone from his handsome features. She tried to ignore it and concentrate on the anguish she'd suffered. "I heard that Camille was here the other night—at your invitation."

"I said I could explain that."

"I shared my deepest insecurities with you, and they meant nothing." Carrie knew that dredging up everything now was unfair, but she couldn't help herself. Camille was so pretty, Carrie couldn't blame Shane if he fell in love with her. But he didn't have to do it so soon.

"Everything you shared with me that night meant a great deal. I—"

"I imagine that once you met Camille, you were able to distinguish the difference between us more readily. She really is a beauty, isn't she? And you must admit there's no competition between the two of us."

"Carrie, I'm trying hard to control my temper, but you're making this difficult." He realized that she was terribly hurt and he blamed himself. He'd assumed, wrongly it seemed, that Camille would have explained everything by now.

As she backed down the stairs, Carrie's peripheral vision caught sight of Bob checking his wristwatch. "I don't have the time to talk now."

"I'll contact you later then," Shane said in that calm, reasonable tone she wanted to hate, "when you've had a chance to think things through."

"Fine." For her part, Carrie had expected to feel triumph and satisfaction for pulling off this minor charade for Shane's benefit. Turning away from him, she felt neither.

Being the gentleman, Bob held open her car door for her and closed it once she was safely inside. Carrie noted that Shane remained on the porch long after they'd pulled out of the driveway. Long after they were out of the sight of his house, Carrie could still feel his eyes searing straight through her.

"Well, how did it go?" Bob asked, his voice keen with curiosity. "Did you bring him up short and surprise him?"

"I'm sure I did."

"Are you sorry we're doing this?"

"I don't know," she told him truthfully. "But I have the feeling it's going to work far better on Camille than Shane."

"I hope so," he grumbled, then stopped abruptly. "I didn't mean that the way it sounded. I'm anxious to get this settled with Camille. Thirty isn't that far away, and I'd like to start a family."

"That may frighten Camille," Carrie commented, recalling her own discussion with her sister on the subject of children.

"I'm not talking about a baseball team here. Just one child, maybe two. Camille wouldn't even have to work outside the home if she doesn't want. I make a good living."

By the time Bob had finished talking about his future with Camille, they'd pulled into the parking lot of Billy's restaurant. "You're sure you want to go through with this?" Carrie asked one last time.

"Positive. I don't want her to think I've been crying in my soup since she's been gone." He paused and chuckled, "Actually, I was weeping in scrambled eggs, as I recall."

Billy's was divided into two distinct areas. The restaurant took up a good portion of the floor space and overlooked San Francisco Bay with its large fleet of fishing boats. The cocktail lounge engaged top-class entertainment and included a small dance floor.

"She hasn't wasted any time, has she?" Bob whispered close to Carrie's ear, and nodded toward a table directly across the room from them. Almost instantly, Carrie found her twin sister.

Now that she'd had the last few days to analyze Camille's behavior, Carrie realized that it wasn't like her sister to jump quite so freely from one relationship to another. Camille was carefree, but not to this extent. Carrie more easily understood her sister's behavior the night of the awards dinner. Camille's search for happiness had been almost desperate that evening. Carrie had indeed been trapped in a web of insecurities not to have noticed it earlier. If Camille danced with Shane and held him too tight, it must've been because she was pretending to be in Bob's arms. If her smile was overly bright, then it was to hide the pain of having lost Bob.

Tonight, Carrie noted that Camille was with another man, seeking to erase the hurt.

"Bob, will you excuse me a minute?"

"Sure," he murmured and Carrie wondered if he'd even heard her. He couldn't take his eyes from Camille. Those two were so much in love that Carrie couldn't allow this charade to continue. Nor was she willing to cause her only sister any additional pain.

Without telling Bob what she was doing, she wove her way around the tables. She heard him softly call her name, not understanding her ploy.

"Hello, Camille," Carrie said, reaching her sister's table. Camille's male companion stood and shook Carrie's hand, introducing himself. Carrie didn't catch the name.

"This is my sister," Camille said stiffly as means of explanation.

"I'm pleased to meet you, Carrie. Would you care to join us?"

"Carrie appears to have her own date." Camille's voice dipped softly, but couldn't disguise the surprise of seeing her sister with Bob.

"Could I talk to you a minute?" Carrie asked.

"Alone?" Camille's eyes met her date's.

"I was just thinking about checking out the cocktail lounge and see what's keeping our drinks," Camille's companion said, rising from his seat.

The moment the man was gone, Carrie took the empty chair. "How did it go with Shane last night?"

"Fine. What are you doing here with Bob?" Camille hissed and leaned forward slightly. Straightening, she folded her hands in her lap like a polite schoolgirl.

"He loves you."

Camille's short laugh bordered on hysterical. "You've got to be kidding. I tested him and he failed. If he honestly loved me—"

"He had a diamond ring in his pocket the night you said you thought that you ought to cool things down a bit."

"A diamond?" Camille's gaze softened as it flew across the restaurant to Bob, who remained standing in the reception area. "He was going to ask me to marry him?" She jerked her head back to study Carrie as though searching for any signs of dishonesty. "Then why didn't he simply tell me so?"

"Pride. The same kind of pride that prevented me from listening to your telephone message this morning. But I want to know now. I need to know."

"Know what?"

"Why did Shane contact you?"

"Oh, he gave me the painting. He said that . . . you should probably ask him why." Ever so slightly, as though being pulled by a powerful magnet, Camille's eyes returned to Bob. "Are you sure Bob's telling you the truth?"

"I'm sure." Carrie felt like the world's biggest fool. Naturally Shane wouldn't want the portrait any longer. Not when he knew the painting was of Camille and not her. She'd forgotten that completely. But she didn't have time to deal with her own foolishness now. Camille's happiness was at stake. "Bob came to me today a broken man because he'd lost you. He loves you."

Carrie was convinced her sister hardly heard her. "I thought I'd cry when he agreed to my crazy scheme," Camille murmured. "Then he suggested we ought to make this cooling off period permanent and I wanted to die. For weeks I'd been thinking about being a wife and you know what?" She didn't wait for a response. "I know I'm going to like it. I've even given some thought to having children. I wouldn't mind being a mother if I could have Bob's babies."

"If you went to him, I think you two could solve this misunderstanding."

"Maybe." The shield of pride was quickly erected.

"Maybe!" Carrie echoed. "Don't be a fool. The man you love is waiting on the other side of this room for you. If you've got so much pride that you can't go to him, then I think you deserve to lose him." Standing, Carrie pushed the chair back. "I can't do anything more for either of you. In fact, I've got my own bridges to mend." She smiled gently at her sister. "It seems we've discovered love together. Let's not be stupid enough to throw away something this precious."

Camille's hand around her wrist stopped her. "You're going to Shane?"

"Yes, and not a minute too soon."

They exchanged encouraging looks. "Good luck."

"You too."

As Carrie sauntered past Bob, she winked and quirked her head toward Camille. "Everything's settled. I know you'll be a fantastic brother-in-law."

Instantly Bob's countenance brightened, and his eyes softened with love as his gaze locked with Camille's. Carrie didn't stay to watch the lovers' reunion.

A taxi was waiting outside the restaurant, and Carrie climbed in the back seat and gave the driver Shane's address. She only hoped that she wasn't too late and that he was home.

The taxi ride seemed to take an eternity. All the way there, Carrie rehearsed what she planned to say. There was always the comical approach. She would tell him that dating Bob was all a joke—which it was, in a way. Then there was the "pretend nothing was wrong" angle. But she didn't know how successful that would be. Honesty would work best, but admitting what a fool she'd been wouldn't be easy.

The cab stopped in front of Shane's house. The light shining from his living room window was encouraging. At least he was home. She had visions of working up her courage and coming this far only to have the house empty.

Carrie paid the driver and told him he needn't wait for her. The sound of the cab driving away echoed in her ear as she stood outside Shane's front door.

A full five minutes passed before she had courage enough to ring the doorbell. Another minute came and went until he finally appeared.

Finding Carrie standing there was a shock. All evening he'd been planning what he wanted to say to her. It was apparent that they had a terrible communication problem.

"Hello, Shane." Her smile was falsely cheerful.

Shane looked around her. "Are you alone this time?" His tone was more gruff than he'd intended.

"Yes. I guess I should apologize for that. I saw Camille and she explained about the painting . . . well, you know."

"Yes, I do know."

"May I come in?" This was even worse than she'd imagined.

"If you'd like." He stepped aside and followed her into his home, indicating that she should go to the sitting room on her right.

She saw that he'd put up the portrait she delivered that evening. Seeing it caught her by surprise. "It looks nice."

"I'll tell the artist." His features softened perceptively.

"I want to apologize for my atrocious behavior earlier."

"I figured as much," he said and rubbed his hand along the back of his neck. "You're needlessly insecure."

"You certainly didn't do anything to help me overcome that," Carrie flung back, angry with him for making this so damned difficult. "One day I bare my soul and the next thing I know you're dating my sister."

"Meeting her is a far cry from dating."

"Not in my book. Surely you must have known she'd tell me. What would it have cost you to let me know your plans?" She knew she sounded like an unreasonable shrew, but she was embarrassed and angry. She'd expected that this meeting wouldn't be easy, but she hadn't thought Shane would be the one to make it so unpleasant.

"I expected you to trust me."

"From past experience with men, I find that difficult."

"What do I have to do to help you to trust me?" He threw the words at her.

His raised voice caused her to grimace. "Well, trust is something special. It's not like we're engaged or anything."

"Engaged? You mean we have to be married before I'm entitled to your trust? Is that what you mean?"

"I..."

"This sounds a lot like a marriage proposal. Is that what you're suggesting?"

At the end of her patience, Carrie tossed her hands in the air. "I don't know. No. Yes."

"Fine then."

Chapter Nine

F ine what?'' Carrie stared at him blankly.

"We'll get married.''

Carrie was astonished that she'd answered such an outrageous question so flippantly. Stunned that Shane treated the subject so lightly. And furious with them both.

"You don't seem very happy,'' he commented, his look dark and intense.

Carrie's face was flushed; her eyes wide with shock. "When?'' The feeble voice hardly sounded like her own. He'd handed her an answer to her insecurities and she jumped on it.

"Three months,'' Shane said next.

This isn't right, her conscience accused. Marriage was sacred. A blending of hearts and souls. A linking of two lives, intertwining personalities, goals, ambitions, destinies. Good heavens, this wasn't some silly game. It was their very lives they were treating so off-handedly. She should never have agreed...but yet she loved Shane. It shouldn't matter that she was the one to offhandedly approach the subject. He'd agreed of his own free will. He wanted this, too. Now wasn't the time to question his motives.

"Well?" he asked. "Does three months give you enough time?"

"Yes." Once again she replied in a low, shaking tone. She couldn't quite believe this was real. She felt as if she were intoxicated. Her head spun and a queasy sensation attacked her stomach. "I'll be a good wife to you, Shane."

"What about children?"

"Children? I haven't given the subject much thought."

"Well, if we're going to be married it's something we're going to need to discuss sooner or later."

"I agree."

"I know your art is important to you. I want you to realize that if you have my baby, you won't have to give up the things you love."

From his response, Carrie realized that Shane thought she didn't want a family. "I love children and...I'll love having yours." The words stumbled over each other in her eagerness to assure him. "It's just that I'm having trouble accepting that all this is happening."

"Believe it."

"Then you feel we should start a family right away?"

Shane chuckled, bringing her into his arms. His look was faintly amused. "I think we'd best hold off until after the wedding, don't you?"

"All right." Carrie hardly realized what she was agreeing to.

His arms tightened around her waist, bringing her even closer. "In case you didn't know it, I want you, Carrie Lockett. Desperately." His voice was as smooth as satin. Husky. Sexy. Romantic.

Carrie's eyes drifted closed. This was too good to be true. She'd wake up in another hour and discover it had all been a delicious dream. But when Shane's warm mouth found hers, the sensations that flooded her were far too real to be imaginary. His touch left her dazed and uncoordinated. Shell-shocked. She was drunk with love!

"We should tell someone," Shane whispered against her neck, continuing to spread tiny, biting kisses down the slope of her throat.

"Who?"

"My great-aunt."

"And Elizabeth Brandon," Carrie suggested. After all, it was Elizabeth who was responsible for getting them together. "And Camille."

"Should I talk to your father?"

"Dad? Why?"

"Isn't that the way these things are usually done?"

"I...don't know." Unexpectedly this wedding idea was becoming complicated. "Dad would like to meet you."

"No doubt."

"He lives in Sacramento," Carrie explained.

"Should we phone him?" Shane asked.

"It's late now. He's probably already in bed."

Shane growled close to her ear. "Don't mention the word bed to me. It's going to be hell keeping my hands off you for the next three months."

"That long?" Carrie murmured.

"All right, two months."

Carrie didn't realize she'd agreed to such a long wait. Shane could change his mind. He could call everything off at the last minute. He could want out and she wouldn't blame him.

"Could we hurry things along?" she murmured.

"Brilliant idea. When?"

"Two weeks!"

"Oh Lord, I want you, Carrie. What about tomorrow?"

For an instant she honestly considered it, until she realized he had to be teasing. "Two weeks."

"If you insist." He curved a hand around the back of her neck and leaned over to kiss her again. "You have the sweetest mouth."

"Thank you."

"You know what I think?" He spoke even as he kissed the corner of her lips.

"What?"

"If we're planning to go through with this in two weeks' time, we need to talk to our families soon."

"Right."

"I'm going to phone Aunt Ashley." The conversation was momentarily interrupted by a lengthy kiss.

"Now?" Carrie asked once she'd surfaced.

"Right now." He reached behind her for the phone on his desk, punching out the number as he continued kissing her.

Carrie could hear the phone ring as the line connected. When his aunt answered, Shane abruptly broke off the kiss. He continued to hold Carrie in his arms, his eyes smiling into hers.

"It's Shane," he said into the receiver.

Faintly, Carrie could hear his aunt's voice coming over the wire. "Is something wrong?"

"Something's very right. Carrie and I are going to be married."

"That's wonderful news. When?"

Carrie grinned at the delight the older woman's voice revealed. "Soon. Two weeks, I think."

"Two weeks! Why, that's impossible," Ashley continued. "Your sisters will never forgive you if they aren't invited to the wedding."

"Naturally we'll invite them," Shane countered.

"But they can't drop everything on such short notice. Caroline's baby is only a year old."

"Yes, yes, I know," Shane grumbled.

"Tell her we'll schedule the wedding later if it's more convenient," Carrie whispered in his ear, distracting him.

"Aunt Ash, hold on. Carrie's saying something." He covered the telephone receiver with his hand and kissed her on the bridge of her nose. "Have I told you that I love your freckles?"

"No." She felt the heat seep into her cheeks and knew that the freckles would soon switch to their glowing stage.

"According to Aunt Ashley, two weeks is out of the question. We would offend half my family if we don't give them proper notice. It looks like we may be in for a longer wait than we'd originally planned."

"How long?"

"It might be best if we go back to what we first thought—three months."

Carrie managed to control the alarm that filled her. Surely in that length of time, Shane would find a reason to call off the wedding. It took all her willpower to nod in agreement. "That'll be fine."

Shane uncovered the mouthpiece and placed the telephone receiver against his ear. "Three months Aunt Ash?"

"Much better. Can I talk to Carrie?"

Shane handed her the phone. "My aunt wants to talk to you."

Carrie accepted the phone and paused to clear her throat. "Hello."

"Carrie, dear," Ashley Wallingford said warmly. "This is fantastic news. Welcome to the family."

"Thank you. I'm very pleased." Shane made coherent conversation nearly impossible. While she was speaking, he kissed the side of her neck, his lips nibbling upward toward her earlobe. Delicious shivers shot up and down her spine. Carrie thought her knees would give out from under her.

"I realize you and Shane have lots to discuss. We can talk tomorrow. I just wanted you to know that I'm willing to help any way I can."

"Thank you. I'll remember that." Shane located the tiny pearl buttons to her blouse and began unfastening them one by one.

"We'll talk soon, then."

"Soon," Carrie repeated.

"Good night, dear, and tell that rascal of a nephew of mine that I'm exceptionally pleased with his choice."

"I will."

The line disconnected. Carrie managed to swallow a groan as Shane's hand slipped inside her lacy bra. She was delirious with longing. She continued to hold on to the phone as if gripping the appliance would grant her strength.

As Shane caressed her breasts, Carrie laid back her head, rolling it from side to side. Only when she dropped the telephone receiver did Shane give pause.

"Oh Lord, Carrie," he groaned. He wrapped his arms around her. "Waiting for you is going to be hell."

"I love you," she cried, urgently squeezing her arms around his neck. "I love you so much." Tears rained down her face. She couldn't get enough of him. Couldn't press herself close enough to satisfy the longings of her heart.

"I'd better take you home while I've still got the strength."

As they drove to the beach house, Shane hummed along with the music playing on the radio. His mood was glorious. Hers was weighted down wondering if they were basing the most important decision of their lives on over-excited hormones.

Once at the beach house, Shane leaned over and kissed her lightly. He kept the car engine running while he walked her to the front door. When Carrie revealed her surprise, he explained.

"That's my insurance." His kiss was reverent. "This way I won't be tempted to haul you into that house and cart you off to the bedroom."

Carrie stood transfixed, unable to speak. Her mind was awhirl with doubts. She'd been angry when she'd answered his question regarding the marriage proposal. Flippant. Never in a hundred years had she expected Shane to agree. But he had, and now things were out of control.

He lowered his head, bringing his face inches from hers. His lips gave her a feather-light kiss. "Night, love."

"Night." He straightened and took a step back.

Carrie's world came crashing down with the impact of a nuclear warhead. He hadn't once said he loved her. He'd only spoken of desire. Any love had been implied. He probably wasn't aware he hadn't told her. Maybe he didn't because he was too honest a person to lie. Maybe he had confused desire with love and assumed that since he wanted her so much that he would learn to love her.

Long after Shane had left, Carrie stood on the porch. Her mind was fuzzy. She didn't know what to do.

She'd sleep on it, she decided, holding back a yawn. In the morning everything would be clear and she'd know what she should do.

Painting was impossible. All morning Carrie tried to occupy her mind with her art, but to no avail. At noon, she gave up the effort. As she cleaned her equipment, she sorted through her thoughts. She needed to talk to someone. She toyed with the idea of contacting Elizabeth Brandon, but decided against calling the art dealer. The one person who readily came to mind was Camille, but Carrie wasn't entirely convinced she could trust her twin sister. Sad, but true. They were so different. Camille was water, shimmering and changing. Carrie was the earth, stable and secure. Together, they made mud.

Undecided, Carrie changed from her faded jeans into a pale pink dress. If she was going to talk to anyone, it would have to be Camille. They may not be alike, but they had gotten along better these last few weeks than at any other time in their lives. Camille always came to Carrie with her worries and anxieties. For the first time ever, Carrie was going to Camille.

After a brief telephone conversation with her sister to verify that they could meet, Carrie left the house, determined to tell Camille everything. She would start at the beginning when Elizabeth Brandon mentioned Shane and how attracted she'd been to him that first day. Carrie would be forthright, she decided. She'd tell Camille how she'd fought the attraction, knowing that if Shane bought *No Competition* he'd probably be drawn more to Camille than to her. But those problems had been solved, and others cropped up faster than Carrie could handle. Now she was engaged to a man, and yet she wasn't entirely convinced he loved her.

Camille was waiting for her in a seafood restaurant close to her office.

"Hi. You look like hell."

Carrie took the chair across from her sister. Camille had never learned the art of tact. "Thanks, I needed that."

Camille seemed genuinely contrite. "I didn't mean anything."

Carrie waved the apology aside with a flick of her wrist. "Don't worry about it. How did things go with Bob last night?"

Camille's happy smile said it all. "Wonderful. We've decided to get married." She held out her left hand for Carrie to admire the beautiful solitaire diamond.

"It's lovely. Congratulations."

"What about you and Shane?"

"We're engaged, too." Carrie didn't need to be told that she revealed none of the happiness that was so obvious in her sister.

"Congratulations," Camille said, but her eyes narrowed and her perfectly shaped mouth thinned slightly. Knowing her sister, Carrie recognized the expression as one of doubt.

"What's wrong?" Carrie decided to meet the question head on.

Camille shook her head. "You don't look pleased."

The waitress came. Carrie hadn't bothered to glance at the menu. There was no reason to. Her sister would probably order what she would have chosen anyway. Camille gave the waitress her selection of French onion soup and a fresh green salad and Carrie seconded it.

"We've been doing a lot of that lately. Have you noticed?"

Carrie had.

"I can't understand it," Camille continued. A tiny frown marred the smooth perfection of her face. "We fought like cats and dogs the whole time we were growing up. Sometimes you were so damned perfect that I thought I hated you.''

"Hated me?" It was so close to her own feelings that Carrie was too stunned to respond. For years, she'd felt totally lacking compared to Camille. Her sister was the angelic ideal.

Carrie interrupted her troubled thoughts. "I wasn't the gorgeous one. You took all the glory for that.'' She revealed only a hint of the bitterness she'd held on to all these years.

Slowly Camille shook her head from side to side, the lovely dark curls brushing the top of her shoulders. "I can't believe I'm hearing this. I had to play up what little beauty I had to make up for the fact you were 'the gifted one.' And you were more than just smart. You had this incredible artistic talent. All my life the only thing I had to compensate with was my face.''

Carrie remained speechless for a full minute. "You were jealous because I did well in school?"

"Uncontrollably.''

"But all my life I've envied you your beauty.''

"Good looks are superficial. No one knows that better than me. I'm a beauty consultant, remember?''

A loud clap of thunder or a surging bolt of lightning couldn't have had more impact. Her gorgeous twin sister had been jealous of her! Carrie was floored.

"All these years we've been competing against each other?''

From her startled look, this information had jarred Camille as well. "It seems so.''

"I can't believe this. Camille, you're warm, loving, generous and a lot of fun.''

"I agree," she concurred with little lack of modesty. "But I didn't make the honor roll once."

"No, you were the homecoming queen when I had to scrounge the bottom of the barrel for a date." Carrie swallowed down a laugh. Two days before the big dance, she'd been asked by the least popular boy in the entire school. Camille had been dating the quarterback of the football team.

"Didn't you go to the prom with Tom Shell?"

"Right. His athletic prowess was on the golf course as I recall." In other words, he wasn't a muscle-bound, popular quarterback.

They broke into simultaneous giggles. Carrie felt like crying and laughing at the same time. It was as if she'd been informed, out of the blue, that she had another twin sister. They'd been separated at birth and hadn't been given the opportunity to meet each other until now, as adults.

"I think you're wonderful, Carrie."

"I feel the same way about you."

"Then why are we always at odds with each other?"

Carrie shook her head with the wonder of it. They'd wasted a lot of years. "Not anymore," she vowed. "There'll be no competition between us, agreed?"

"Agreed." Camille took a long drink from her iced tea. "Now that we're both engaged, what do you think of a double wedding?"

"And let you steal the show?" Carrie joked, but the humor was as artificial as her smile. Her lips trembled with the effort. Soon she was biting into the corner of her mouth to control her unhappiness.

"Carrie, what is it?" Her sister took her hand and squeezed her fingers. "I don't think I've ever seen you cry."

"I do, you know. A lot lately."

"But why?"

"Shane."

"You're engaged. You love him, don't you?"

"Yes," she admitted forcefully. "I love him so much I could die from it."

"I don't believe you need to go to those lengths to prove it."

"Don't joke, Camille. This is serious."

"Sorry." She was instantly contrite. "Now tell me, what's wrong?"

Carrie bowed her head, her fingers shredding the paper napkin into a hundred infinitesimal strips. "I can't, it's too embarrassing."

"I'm your sister!"

It wasn't fair that their newfound understanding had to be tested so quickly. "We may be engaged, but I don't know if he loves me. In fact, I'm not sure who proposed first."

"So, Shane didn't argue, did he?" Camille didn't seem to find anything out of the ordinary. "He couldn't have been opposed to the idea."

"I don't really think he is, but we'd be getting married for all the wrong reasons."

"You love him. What could be so criminal about that?"

Spilling out the story of her various insecurities wouldn't do either of them any good.

"If you have doubts," Camille suggested softly, "then talk to Shane. He loves you."

Carrie thought it best to avoid the subject of Shane for the moment. "Have you and Bob set a date for your wedding?"

"He's seeing what he can do to arrange things quickly. I want you to be my maid of honor."

"I'd love that. And when I get married, you can return the favor." Although at the moment she wasn't sure of her future. "However, I don't doubt that you'll get more attention than the bride."

"You could always carry a small, tasteful watercolor instead of the traditional bridal bouquet," Camille teased. "Once people saw how talented you are, they wouldn't bother to look at me."

They both laughed, free to joke and tease each other for the first time.

From the restaurant, Camille returned to work and Carrie did some shopping, killing time, avoiding the inevitable confrontation with Shane.

She'd hoped to sort out her thoughts while the afternoon passed, but didn't have any success.

Close to Shane's quitting time, Carrie called his office from a pay phone in the foyer of his building. His secretary put her directly through.

"Carrie, love." Shane's greeting was happy, animated. "Where are you? I've been trying to reach you all afternoon."

"Downstairs."

"Great. Come up. Now that we're engaged there are several people you should meet."

Carrie hesitated, not knowing a gracious way to extract herself from the invitation. "Can I do it another time? I look a mess."

"If you like."

"Have you got a moment to talk?" She braced her hand against her forehead and closed her eyes.

"All the time in the world. Do you want to meet me in that cocktail lounge across the street?"

"No—no thanks. I want to talk now."

"Over the phone?"

"It'll be easier this way."

"Carrie, what's wrong?" His voice grew heavy and serious. The exhilaration faded.

"Nothing...everything."

"Where are you? I'll be right down."

"No!" she cried. "Please don't do that. I'm not up to seeing you."

"Why not?"

"I look like hell."

"You couldn't," he said, his tone sincere.

"I must be crazy. I'm head over heels in love with you."

"There's nothing wrong with that, especially since I feel the same way about you."

"Oh Shane, do you really?"

He didn't know what was going on in her tired, confused mind, but he didn't want to leave any room for doubts. "I think the world of you."

"That's going to make what I have to say all the more difficult."

Shane didn't like the sound of this. Not one bit. This woman was unlike anyone he'd ever known. He supposed that was part of what had drawn her to him so fiercely.

"I've been thinking about what happened last night."

"Or what didn't happen?" he teased lovingly. Half the night had been gone before he slept. Leaving her alone on that porch had been damn difficult. Now he wondered if he'd done the right thing.

"Shane, listen to me, because what I have to say is important."

"What is it, love?"

Carrie didn't pause, blurting out the words in one giant breath before she lost her nerve. "I want to call off the wedding."

Chapter Ten

What?'' Shane exploded. "Where are you? I'm coming down right now and we're going to talk about this."

"Shane, listen to me. I apologize. I really do, but I can't go through with it. Goodbye."

"Goodbye! What the hell do you mean by that?"

His question was angrily hurled at her. Carrie heard it loud and clear as she replaced the receiver, disconnecting the pay phone. Her whole body was trembling, but she couldn't see how shouting at each other over the phone, or in person for that matter, would do either of them any good. There didn't seem any point in explaining her reasoning. She couldn't when it remained unclear in her own mind. She needed time to think.

The five o'clock throng of people heading home clogged the sidewalk as Carrie walked outside Shane's office building. She made a sharp left and wove her way in and out of the mass of humanity who all seemed intent on one thing: escaping each other.

She paused at the busy intersection closest to his office to wait for the traffic signal to change. At least Shane admitted caring deeply about her. That was a perk she hadn't anticipated, but then any man who had put up with her craziness as he had these last weeks must hold strong feelings for her.

The light changed and she stepped off the curb. It was then that she heard someone shout her name. She glanced over her shoulder, surprised that Shane had caught up with her in such a short time.

She moved back onto the sidewalk to wait for him. The last thing she wanted was a chase scene reminiscent of some melodramatic television series.

By the time Shane reached her, he was panting, his shoulders heaving with exertion.

His expression was stern, no-nonsense. He was furious, angrier than he could remember being in his life. He couldn't understand this woman. Once he gained his breath, he felt his strength drain out of him. He leaned against the lamppost and shook his head. "Come on," he grumbled. "Let's talk."

"I don't think—"

"For once, Carrie, don't argue with me. I'm not in the mood for it."

He didn't say a word as they trudged the short distance back to his building. The strained silence in the elevator was even worse, if that was possible.

The door to his inner office was wide open in testimony to the urgency of his rush to locate her.

"Sit," he demanded, pointing to the chair in his office.

She did as he asked, but only because she didn't have the energy to defy him.

"All right, talk," he said once he was seated across from her. His desk was the only thing that separated them.

"What do you want me to say?"

"What made you come up with that lunatic decision about calling off the wedding?"

"Insulting me isn't going to help, Shane."

"All right, I apologize. I simply want to know what led to this most recent announcement." Some of the weakness had left his limbs. He wasn't going to let Carrie walk out. He loved her, needed her and in the same instant he wanted to shout at the top of his lungs at her for the anxiety she'd caused him. When he was done with that, he wanted to hold her for an eternity. If Carrie was mixed up, he was doubly so.

Carrie stared at the items on the top of his desk. Anything that prevented her from looking at Shane fascinated her.

"Just explain what happened between last night and this afternoon that caused you to change your mind."

"I . . . I don't know where to start."

"Might I suggest the beginning?" he offered somewhat flippantly.

Carrie shot to her feet. "This is exactly what I mean. This . . . casualness. We were making the most important decision of our lives on a stupid joke."

As he feared, Shane couldn't follow her reasoning. "What do you mean?"

"You...you asked me what you could do to help me to trust you and I blurted out what seemed like a marriage proposal."

"Didn't you mean it?"

"I...I'm not sure. Yes. But that shouldn't matter."

"I agreed, didn't I?"

Carrie was angry all over again. "That's the crux of the problem. It wasn't right."

"Why not?"

"Because you were treating the whole thing like some big joke and it isn't. Marriage is precious."

"I realize that." He was beginning to get the gist of her problem.

"You haven't even said you loved me."

"I love you," he shouted.

"Well, thank you very much. I love you back," she cried in equal volume, whirling around to present him with a clear view of her back. She folded her arms around her waist and swallowed down the hysteria that threatened to choke her. If they both weren't so serious, Carrie could almost laugh at what was happening. They may love each other, but a sea of murky water remained between them.

"Okay, now that we've got that matter cleared up, let's get married."

"No!"

He couldn't believe he'd heard her correctly. "Now what's the problem?"

"First you were being flippant. Now you're angry."

"You're damn right, I'm mad. I don't understand you."

"Are you sure you want to be married to a woman you don't understand?"

"For God's sake, Carrie..."

"Are you swearing at me?"

Shane snapped his mouth shut and clenched his teeth so tightly, his jaw ached. She was so serious he was momentarily speechless. He forced himself to be calm, relaxing the tense muscles of his shoulders. Standing, he joined her at the huge window that overlooked the downtown area. But Shane had no time for the skyscrapers that brushed the edges of the heavens.

"I remember the first time I saw your art," he said, his sober tone rounding off the sharp edges of anger. "It was a seascape. The sky was a pewter color of predawn and the sun was just breaking over the horizon, golden and filled with the promise of a new day. I stared at that painting for ten minutes. I couldn't take my eyes off it. Something about that painting touched me as no painting ever has."

Carrie knew exactly which seascape he was referring to. She'd worked on it for weeks, searching for the proper way to express her feelings. It had been a period of disillusionment in her life. Her father had moved to Sacramento. Carrie and her sister had drifted farther apart than ever, and Carrie had felt like a loner, a recluse. She didn't work with others, her contact with the outside world seemed to be narrowing as she found fewer and fewer interests to share with family and friends.

"I knew then," Shane continued, "that the person who'd painted that seascape had reached deep within herself and triumphed over disenchantment." His smile was a bit crooked. "When I learned that the painting had already been sold, I was disappointed. That was when I asked Elizabeth to call me if something else came in by the same artist."

"I remember the painting," Carrie murmured, not knowing what else to say.

"When Elizabeth contacted me to say there was another seascape of yours available, I told her to consider it sold even without seeing it."

"You did?"

His eyes were unnaturally bright as he nodded sharply. "I wasn't disappointed."

Carrie bowed her head.

"I think I may have even started loving you way back then. A whole year before I followed you on Fisherman's Wharf."

"Shane..."

"No, let me finish. I couldn't understand why you were such a prickly thing. After buying all those paintings of yours, I suppose I felt you owed me something. After all, I thought I knew you so well. It was a shock to have you behave so differently from the way I expected. I don't think I fully understood you until I met Camille."

"We talked today... Camille and I. Really talked. I'm hoping a lot of our problems are over. We aren't competing against each other any more. There'll be no competition between us again."

"I'm glad."

A short silence followed.

"I guess what I'm trying to say," Shane spoke first, "is that I've had an unfair advantage in this relationship. I love you, Carrie, I've loved you for months. It's true that I've probably gone about everything wrong, but I was impatient. I rushed you when I shouldn't have. It isn't any wonder you're filled with questions. I nearly blew this whole thing."

"You didn't do anything wrong," she said softly. "I did."

Tenderly Shane brushed the hair from her temple, then paused, dropping his hand as though he didn't trust himself to touch her. "When you said yes about getting married, I thought great, wonderful. It was what I'd hoped would happen all along."

"I was outraged with myself for treating the subject so lightly. Then I was furious with you for answering me."

"If you hadn't honestly meant it, why didn't you say something at the time?"

Now it was Carrie's turn to swallow her pride. "I meant it...I wanted to be your wife so badly that I was afraid that if I didn't follow through with the marriage now, I may not get another chance."

"Oh, my sweet, confused Carrie."

"And then you started talking about children and I wanted to have your babies so much I was willing to overlook just about anything. I think any children we have will be marvelous."

"Yet you're willing to walk away from all this happiness when it's here waiting for you?"

"I couldn't help it," she cried, her voice only slightly raised. "What else was I to think? You never admitted you loved me. All these weeks I've walked around in fear that once you discovered Camille I would be history. You did buy her portrait. And worse, every time you looked at her, it was like you were worshiping some love goddess."

"I thought it was you."

"I know. But that only made things worse."

"How?" Once again he had problems following her reasoning.

"Because it only made me feel more guilty about deceiving you." Carrie recalled the relief mixed with guilt that she'd suffered those frantic days before Shane found out about Camille.

He turned sideways then, fitting his hands on her shoulders. His long fingers closed over the gentle sloping line of her upper arms. "I've made my own mistakes. Ones I want to undo right now. To simply say 'I love you' doesn't cover what I feel for you, Carrie Lockett. I love everything about you, from that turned-up freckled nose to that yard-wide streak of stubbornness."

The words washed over her like a cooling rain in the driest part of summer. "I think you must honestly love me to put up with me. And I do trust you—with all my heart."

"You think we should consider marriage then?"

"Yes."

"But I'll do the asking this time." His hands dropped from her arms to circle her waist. His eyes grew warm and vital. "I've been waiting a lifetime for you, Carrie. Would you do me the very great honor of being my wife?"

She blinked back the tears that sprang readily to the surface and burned for release. Words were impossible.

"Well?" he prompted.

Her response was to nod wildly and sniffle.

"That better mean yes."

"It does. Now will you stop being such a gentleman and kiss me?"

Shane was only too happy to comply.

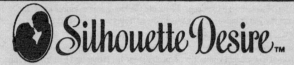

COMING NEXT MONTH

#514—THE THINGS WE DO FOR LOVE—Glenda Sands
When pretty Shelby Thurston offered Austin Hastings ready employment, he was intrigued enough to accept. Little did the handsome engineer know the talents the job entailed. But he would do anything for love—and Shelby.

#515—TO CHOOSE A WIFE—Phyllis Halldorson
Susan Alessandro was a blond angel, but Marco Donatello had never been attracted to innocent romantics, especially one his father had handpicked for him to marry. They had nothing in common—except their growing love for each other.

#516—A DANGEROUS PROPOSITION—Melodie Adams
As an undercover investigator, Blake Marlow was a professional. So why was suspected smuggler Cassandra Wyatt giving him sleepless nights? He should have been able to handle a routine case, but his unexpected feelings for Cassandra were anything but routine.

#517—MAGGIE MINE—Karen Young
Maggie Taylor believed in love, marriage and happily ever after.
Cash McKenzie was a dyed-in-the-wool cynic, disillusioned with romance. Could Maggie reawaken the romantic in Cash and teach him to love again?

#518—THE BOY NEXT DOOR—Arlene James
Ronni Champlain still cringed at the memory of her adolescent crush on Jeff Paul Logan, and she was determined to stay away from him. But when her little sister started to gaze at him with hero-worship in her eyes, Ronni knew she had to step in. Could she save her sister, or would Ronni soon fall back under Jeff Paul's magical spell?

#519—MR. LONELYHEARTS—Suzanne Forster
When Scott "The Hunter" Robinson refused to notice Amy Dwyer, she wrote to her paper's advice column for help. She was surprised to find that Hunter was the new columnist! Soon, Amy was following his advice—right into his heart.

AVAILABLE THIS MONTH:

#508 ONE OF THE FAMILY
Victoria Glenn

#509 TANGLED TRIUMPHS
Terri Herrington

#510 A MIST ON THE MOUNTAIN
Stella Bagwell

#511 PERFECT PARTNERS
Jennifer Mikels

#512 NO COMPETITION
Debbie Macomber

#513 ON RESTLESS WINGS
Mia Maxam